Roscommon County Library

LEABHARLANN CHONTAE ROSCOMAIN

This book should be returned not later than the last date shown below. It may be renewed if not requested by another borrower.

Books are on loan for 14 days from the date of issue.

305528 (4)

F|LP

DATE DUE	DATE DUE	DATE DUE	DATE DUE
11. MAR, 05,			
25. MAR, 05,			
29. APR 05,			
04. JUN 05.			

D1340408

SPECIAL MESSAGE TO READERS

This book is published under the auspices of

THE ULVERSCROFT FOUNDATION

(registered charity No. 264873 UK)

Established in 1972 to provide funds for research, diagnosis and treatment of eye diseases. Examples of contributions made are: —

A Children's Assessment Unit at Moorfield's Hospital, London.

•

Twin operating theatres at the Western Ophthalmic Hospital, London.

•

A Chair of Ophthalmology at the Royal Australian College of Ophthalmologists.

•

The Ulverscroft Children's Eye Unit at the Great Ormond Street Hospital For Sick Children, London.

You can help further the work of the Foundation by making a donation or leaving a legacy. Every contribution, no matter how small, is received with gratitude. Please write for details to:

THE ULVERSCROFT FOUNDATION,
The Green, Bradgate Road, Anstey,
Leicester LE7 7FU, England.
Telephone: (0116) 236 4325

In Australia write to:
THE ULVERSCROFT FOUNDATION,
c/o The Royal Australian and New Zealand
College of Ophthalmologists,
94-98 Chalmers Street, Surry Hills,
N.S.W. 2010, Australia

HUNT FOR GOLD

Cashiered from the army, Major Cobb, along with other men, is hired to escort a shipment of gold. However, what they think will be a routine task proves to be very different when there is a failed attempt to rob them of the gold. Then comes the revelation that it isn't gold, but just sand. Now Cobb is hired as a deputy US marshal to hunt down those responsible, but he faces death at every step of the way. He will need all his skills to uncover the truth.

Roscommon County Library Service

WITHDRAWN
FROM STOCK

Roscommon County Library Service

WITHDRAWN
FROM STOCK

FRANK FIELDS

HUNT FOR GOLD

Complete and Unabridged

LINFORD
Leicester

First published in Great Britain in 2003 by
Robert Hale Limited
London

First Linford Edition
published 2004
by arrangement with
Robert Hale Limited
London

The moral right of the author has been asserted

Copyright © 2003 by Frank Fields
All rights reserved

British Library CIP Data

Fields, Frank
    Hunt for gold.—Large print ed.—
Linford western library
    1. Western stories
    2. Large type books
    I. Title
    823.9'14 [F]

    ISBN 1–84395–514–8

395528(4)
ROSCOMMON
F|AP

Published by
F. A. Thorpe (Publishing)
Anstey, Leicestershire
Set by Words & Graphics Ltd.
Anstey, Leicestershire
Printed and bound in Great Britain by
T. J. International Ltd., Padstow, Cornwall

This book is printed on acid-free paper

1

The only thing Cobb wanted after his long trek across what was little more than desert, was a bit of peace and quiet and a drink, but it was at that precise moment that the only other customer of the saloon decided to attach himself to him.

The man was plainly very drunk but appeared far from being incapable. Cobb looked hard at him and decided that discretion was better than trying to make the man go away, since he did not think that he would be able to reason with the man in his present condition, if he could ever be reasoned with.

The drunk was a big man, at least four inches taller than Cobb's six foot and a bit and appeared almost as broad across his shoulders as his height. He was certainly not a man to be messed with and Cobb was not really the type to pick a fight with anyone. True, he was more than capable of looking after himself both in a fist fight or a gunfight with most men should the need arise. Whilst he could undoubtedly have handled his unwelcome guest had it come to using his gun, he had serious doubts as to whether or not his fists would have made even the slightest impression on the man-mountain now demanding that he should buy him a drink.

'I seen you ride into town,' the drunk leered at him. 'Yep, I says to myself, he looks like the kind of man what'd buy another man a drink. I got me a nose for these things. I can allus tell when a man is the friendly type. Mine's a beer.'

'And I'll bet you don't have many friends round here or anywhere else for that matter,' said Cobb. 'Looking at you I'd say you've already had enough to drink and it's early in the day yet.'

'Sure, I got me lots of friends,' said the drunk. He looked around the saloon which was empty apart from the two of them. 'You're right, it's a bit early for them though. You'll see, when they do come in the first thing they'll do is buy me a drink. Yes, sir, I got me lots of friends. As for havin' had enough, don't you worry none about me, I can take it. Yes, sir, you ask anyone in these parts an' they'll all tell you Sam Coltrane sure can take his liquor.'

Cobb looked at the bartender who nodded and leaned over the counter to whisper in his ear.

'Sure, he can take it,' said the bartender. 'He's an expert at takin' drinks off anybody who happens to be in here. There's not that many who are prepared to argue with him.'

'That's what I thought,' Cobb whispered in reply. 'I'd say he doesn't take too kindly to anyone who refuses either.'

'Mister,' said the bartender, 'it just ain't worth the bother, believe me. I'd buy him a drink if I was you and then make an excuse to get out of here. If you don't go he'll be badgerin' you all the time.'

'OK,' said Cobb turning to the drunk, 'beer it is.'

'There speaks a true gentleman,' said Coltrane, as he snatched at the glass of beer which was placed in front of him. 'Your very good health, sir.'

Cobb smiled, paid for the beer, finished his own drink and then made to leave the saloon. 'I've got a few things to do,' he said to the bartender. 'Is there a hotel or rooming-house in town?'

'Both,' replied the bartender. 'There's the Hotel Majestic just along the street opposite the church an' there's a roomin'-house further down next door to the general store. The roomin'-house is straw on hard bunks, but the bedbugs ain't quite so savage in the hotel and the room service is far superior.'

That last remark about being far superior room service was followed by a wry smile but its meaning was lost on Cobb.

'Hey!' called the drunk, 'You only just got here. Why you leavin' so soon?'

'I only needed a drink to lay the dust in my throat,' said Cobb. 'Now I need a bath and to find somewhere to sleep the night.'

'Bath!' exclaimed the drunk. 'Bathin' ain't healthy. I ain't had me a bath in years an' look at me, it ain't done me no harm.'

'I can smell that,' said Cobb. He raised his hand to the bartender. 'Maybe I'll see you later. It all depends on how crowded you are.' He looked meaningfully at Sam Coltrane.

The bartender nodded, plainly understanding Cobb's meaning. 'It usually gets less crowded round about nine,' he said.

Cobb went outside and was relieved when Coltrane didn't follow him. He led his horse along the street and looked at the peeling paintwork on the outside of the Hotel Majestic for a few moments. Majestic was hardly the name he would have given it, but it

5

appeared reasonably clean and had the added attraction of a very good-looking woman behind the small reception desk.

'How much for one night?' Cobb asked her from the open doorway.

She looked up and smiled broadly at him. 'For me or the room?' she asked. 'You can have both if you want.'

'I thought this was a hotel not a whorehouse,' said Cobb.

'It is,' said the woman. 'Like any good hotel we also offer extra room service for those who want it.'

The significance of the bartender's remark now made sense, but he was still very surprised.

'I take it you've got no man about,' said Cobb.

'There's lots of men about,' said the woman, 'but if you are meaning do I have a husband, the answer is no. He up and left me more than two years ago. He could be dead now for all I know or care.'

'OK, I get the picture,' said Cobb.

'How much just for the room?'

'One dollar a night, five dollars for seven days,' she said. 'Room service is another two dollars a night or ten dollars for seven days.'

'A dollar a night seems a bit steep for a place out here in the middle of nowhere,' said Cobb. 'I'll have to think about it.'

'Don't think too long,' she said, 'rooms go pretty fast.'

'Sure, I can see everyone lining up along the street,' Cobb said sarcastically. 'I'll think about it.'

'Well there's nowhere else apart from the roomin'-house,' she said. 'He might be cheaper but all you get is a rough blanket, a few boards for a bunk, straw to lie on and as many bedbugs as you like. Here I provide clean sheets, a proper mattress and the only bedbugs are those you might bring in yourself. Anyhow, you can only have a room for two nights at the most.'

'Two nights? OK, I'll still think about it,' said Cobb. 'Right now I'm not too flush with money.' He did not ask why he could have the room for two nights only since he had no real intention of staying that long.

He did not give her the opportunity to reply and continued along the street until he came to a rather large but very rickety-looking shack with a rough, hand-painted sign outside proclaiming it to be the rooming-house. A smaller sign underneath gave the price of one night's stay as 25¢ and a full week at $1.50.

There was no need for him to go in, there were more than enough gaps between the wall boards to see what was on offer inside. He felt in his shirt pocket, pulled out two grubby notes and, smoothing them out, decided that in this case he would be better off spending his money at the hotel.

Finding livery for his horse presented no problem. He had seen a livery stable along the small street at the side of the church and soon had his horse bedded down with good feed and water. Whilst he was prepared to spend almost any amount ensuring that his horse was well fed and cared for, he still begrudged spending a dollar a night on himself at that moment.

'How about fifty cents a night,' he said to the woman in the Hotel Majestic when he went back.

She leaned on the small counter and stared up at him, smiled, and then shook her head.

'You know, I must've got you all wrong, mister,' she said. 'I had you down as a better class of man than we usually get round here. I thought you might appreciate a good bed and even a good woman. Although I say so myself you won't find a better woman than me. Seems I was wrong though. You're even tighter-assed than most and most men round here have asses tighter than a duck's and nothin' gets through that, not even water.'

'Seventy-five cents,' offered Cobb, ignoring her remarks. 'And no room service.'

'OK, mister, seventy-five cents it is,' she sighed, holding her hand out for the money. 'That's in advance. It's not that I don't trust you, but I've had customers who have skipped out early in the mornin' without payin'. A girl sure isn't goin' to get rich with the likes of you, is she?'

'Does that include a dinner and breakfast?' he asked.

'What the hell do you expect for your money?' she demanded. 'Food I can give you, but that's extra an' strictly cash in advance. I can do you a beef stew for dinner at fifty cents and ham an' eggs in the mornin' for fifty cents. Take it or leave it, no haggling, no bargaining. If you want food tonight and in the mornin', that'll be one dollar seventy-five. No cash in advance, no room and no food.'

'You drive a hard bargain,' Cobb said mockingly, as he counted out the money.

'*I* drive a hard bargain!' she said with a derisive laugh. 'Mister, you're lucky this is a slack week. In two days it'll be a different story. The town will be full of miners then, all only too eager to spend as much as they can of their hard-earned cash. All my rooms will be taken and my room service will be on overtime. I'll even have to take on help.'

'Miners?' queried Cobb. 'It doesn't look like mining country to me. Where are they?'

'Up in Yuma Valley, about twenty-five miles away,' she said. 'They come into town once a month for a few days to sell their gold. You probably saw the state assay wagon on your way in. They come here once a month an' buy the miners' gold, an' then the miners come in here and the saloon to spend all their cash. It's a nice arrangement.'

'They must keep you very busy,' said Cobb. 'I didn't see a whorehouse as I came in. I would have thought that would be the first thing the miners wanted.'

'It is,' she said with a dry laugh. 'That's what I meant about me havin' to take on help. I've got me ten rooms and for them few days they're in use all the time, day and night.'

'Where does your help come from?' he asked.

'You know, mister,' she said mockingly, 'as well as bein' a tightwad you're very nosy but I'd say you were an educated man. In fact you're obviously such a refined gentleman that I don't think you would understand or believe me.'

'Try me,' he said.

'What did you see as you came into town?' she asked. 'I'll tell you what you saw. You saw a lot of piss-poor scrub land with a few homesteads and farms. Most of those farms can hardly scrape a livin' so most of the women head for town once a month when the miners are in town. They don't necessarily all do it at once, they come in maybe two months out of three, but there's more'n enough of them to keep the miners happy.'

'You mean . . . Don't their menfolk mind?'

'Don't their menfolk mind!' she exclaimed. 'Mister, in most cases it's their menfolk who insist that their women do it. In three days, maybe four at the most, most women can earn upwards of a hundred and fifty dollars, some far more than that. That kind of money can buy a lot of food and clothes or anythin' else the women want and as much whiskey as their menfolk can manage. No, sir, their menfolk sure don't mind.'

'And I suppose you rent out your rooms to these women,' said Cobb. 'It's probably a good earner for you as well.'

'There you go again,' she said, laughing at him. 'Bein' nosy. Sure, it helps make ends meet. Now, do you want the stew and the ham and eggs or not? You could try up the street, there's an eatin'-house there which the miners all use. The food isn't worth eatin' though, mostly turnips, turnip greens and meat which is more gristle than anythin' else. That's what they get for breakfast as well. Still, the miners don't seem to mind. I suppose that's because most of them are too drunk to notice what they eat.'

'OK, I'll take the stew and ham and eggs,' agreed Cobb. 'Tell me which room and I'll take my things up.'

'I wouldn't leave that rifle where it can be seen,' she said. 'Things like that have a nasty habit of goin' missin'.'

'Thanks for the warning,' said Cobb.

'First floor, room two, overlookin' the street,' said the woman. 'Dinner will be about six o'clock if that's all right.' She handed him a key.

Cobb nodded and went up to the room which seemed clean and comfortable enough. He looked out of the window from where he had a good view of most of the small town. He was surprised that it appeared larger than he had first imagined it to be, but it was still quite small.

A little further up the street he could see the sheriff's office, next door to which was another office bearing the name 'Assay Office'. Two men were moving things into this office from a wagon. A little further along was a barber's shop and in places such as this Cobb knew that the barber usually also provided hot baths and he felt he needed a good bath.

Heeding the woman's advice, he looked for a place to hide his rifle. He found a loose floorboard under the bed which looked as though it had been used for just such a purpose many times. Since there was nowhere else and because he did not want to carry it around with him, he slipped it and some ammunition into the space beneath. He then went out on to the street.

As he had expected, the barber did provide baths and he was just in the process of changing his prices for baths, haircuts and shaves on a board outside his shop. Cobb stood behind him as he altered the prices from 50¢ to $10 for a hair cut, from 25¢ to $5 for a beard trim and from 50¢ to $10 for a bath.

'Ten dollars for a bath!' Cobb

exclaimed. 'Why the sudden increase in prices? Surely there's nobody prepared to pay that much.'

'Day after tomorrow they'll be queuein' for them,' said the barber.

'Oh, I see,' said Cobb, 'the miners. I want a bath now though. I hope you don't expect me to pay ten dollars. I'm not a rich miner.'

The man looked Cobb up and down and nodded. 'I guess not,' he said. 'Today, you can have a bath at the regular price of fifty cents. How about a haircut or a shave?'

'Just the bath,' said Cobb.

It had been at least three weeks since Cobb had had a bath and he really appreciated the soap and hot water. He did consider letting the barber loose on his haircut then thought better of it, even at the normal price of fifty cents. He had had better towels before. But at least it did the job.

When he left the barber's shop, Cobb saw a man pinning a notice on the wall of the assay office. He assumed that it was something to do with the miners and their gold but, simply because he was curious, he read it. To his surprise it was offering work as armed escort to the gold shipment when it left town. It was only three days' work but it offered payment of ten dollars. Being short of cash and having nowhere in particular to go, he decided to ask about it.

'Three days, that's all it is,' explained the man. 'As far as the railroad in Geraldine.' He looked Cobb up and down and nodded. 'What's your name?'

'Cobb,' replied Cobb.

'Cobb!' grunted the man. 'Is that all?'

'That's all,' replied Cobb.

'No given name?' asked the man. 'I'm always suspicious about a man who says he only has one name.'

'Cobb is all I've ever been known as, even when I was in the army.'

'Army!' said the man, raising an eyebrow. 'You know how to obey orders then? You don't look like a common soldier. What rank were you?'

'Major,' replied Cobb. 'A major in

the Corps of Engineers.'

'Major!' The man was plainly surprised. 'I was in the Sixth Cavalry, a captain. What made you give it up — retire?'

'I suppose you could say that,' replied Cobb. 'They certainly didn't need my services any longer.'

The man smiled. 'Cashiered!' he said.

'For striking a fellow officer,' said Cobb.

'Hell, they don't normally cashier an officer just for something like that, at least not if it's a fellow officer,' said the man. 'If you'd hit an enlisted soldier they're more likely to do something like that, but not a fellow officer. What happened?'

'I found him in bed with my wife,' said Cobb.

'Even less reason,' said the man. 'If anyone should have been cashiered it should have been him.'

'Well, they didn't like the fact that I beat him almost to a pulp,' said Cobb. 'I think he had to retire in the end. My case was not helped by the fact that my dear wife refused to admit what had happened and claimed that I beat him up over a gambling debt. It was also not helped by the fact that her brother was also my commanding officer and had never liked the idea of me marrying his sister.'

'OK,' replied the man. 'I guess that might explain a thing or two. How come you're out here and looking for odd jobs like this? With your experience and qualifications you should be able to get a good job easily enough.'

'I suppose I had too many years of moving from place to place,' said Cobb. 'I was in the engineers which meant that I was being sent all over the place at very short notice. I know we had a main base but I was hardly ever there. I suppose I just can't settle down.'

'OK, Major, that's your affair I suppose,' said the man. 'You're hired, in fact you'll be in charge of the party. For that you'll be paid twenty dollars for the three days. You provide your own guns and ammunition, but if you have to fire any shots we'll pay for the bullets.'

'Are you expecting shots to be fired?' asked Cobb.

'No, Major, we are not,' replied the man. 'I've been doing this job for almost three years, going out to places like this and buying gold and so far we haven't had one attempt on us. I'd like to keep it that way as well. And before you ask, no, we don't employ regular guards. They've tried that in one or two places and in every case the guards have ended up stealing the gold. It was decided that even at ten dollars a man it was cheaper to do it this way. So far it's also been safer to use men who don't know each other.'

'I can see why,' said Cobb. 'Most men might dream about stealing the gold but there are very few who would actually go through with it. They might, if they had time to plan it out like your guards did, but on the spur of the moment it remains a dream to most men. It's like shooting a man. There's not many who can actually squeeze that trigger when there's a man in his sights. An animal — yes, a man — no.'

'Could you kill a man?'

'Yes,' replied Cobb firmly.

'Good,' said the man. 'OK, Major Cobb, You're hired. My name's Fisher, Captain John Fisher and although you out-rank me, I'm still in charge.'

'I thought you said I would be in charge of the party?' said Cobb.'

'And so you will be,' said Fisher. 'I can normally get four or five men — I try to get five but that's not always possible. You and the others will take the gold back to Geraldine where you will hand it over to a man from state treasurer's office. The only regular man with you will be the driver of the wagon. I go on to another mining-camp from here, so it's most unlikely we shall ever meet again. You be here at six in the morning on Monday.'

'Monday,' mused Cobb. 'I've got a place to stay tonight and probably tomorrow night, but I'm told my room

Roscommon County Library Ser
WITHDRAWN
FROM STOCK

21

is needed by some whore of a farmer's wife for about three days after that and I sure don't fancy the rooming-house.'

'That means you're staying at the Hotel Majestic,' said Fisher. 'I've heard about that place. Maybe you'd better come to some arrangement with Mary. I'm sure she'll be only too happy to oblige.'

'I'll have to think about it,' said Cobb. 'Money is in short supply at the moment. I don't suppose you pay in advance?'

'No, Major,' said Fisher, 'I do not. That's asking for money to be thrown away. If I did that a lot of men wouldn't turn up.'

'OK, Captain,' said Cobb, seeing the sense of it. 'I'll report for duty at 0-six hundred hours on Monday.'

Cobb felt quite pleased with himself; he had been thinking of finding work for a couple of days, but this was much better than anything he might have been offered. If he had been very lucky, three days of hard labour might have given him six dollars at the most. This way he was being paid for travelling somewhere he would probably have ended up going anyway.

Mary, who apparently owned the Hotel Majestic, served him what proved to be a very good stew and a large mug of coffee, although the coffee was plainly not real. There was nothing unusual in that. Most of the more remote towns usually served up what was known as prairie or desert coffee. This consisted of local herbs, seeds and even grasses. In some places it was thickened by nothing more than sand. This did not appear to have any sand in it.

She was obviously a businesswoman and although she sympathized with Cobb's predicament in having nowhere to stay for two nights, she was not prepared to let him have the room even at the full price of one dollar a night. According to her, she could make $20 a day for each room while the miners were in town.

After he had eaten, Cobb decided to risk having Sam Coltrane attach himself to him and went along to the saloon. As he had expected, it did not take Coltrane very long to find him.

'Mine's a beer!' said Coltrane, giving Cobb a hearty slap on the back. The effect of the slap was to make Cobb cough and choke.

'You need to be more careful,' he complained to Coltrane. 'You don't know your own strength. You could do a man serious damage.'

'I'm celebratin',' said Coltrane, ignoring Cobb's remark. 'I got me some work. Not much, but it pays good. Ten dollars for three days ridin' escort to the gold. I wanted to go to Geraldine anyhow, so I might as well get paid for goin' there.'

'Escorting gold!' said Cobb. He had the distinct feeling that he ought to pull out there and then. He looked up at Coltrane and smiled weakly. 'Good, I'm pleased for you. I don't suppose there's much work around here.'

'Not much,' agreed Coltrane. 'Sometimes I earn a couple of dollars down at the lumber yard an' I dig a grave now an' then, but it ain't regular.'

Cobb decided that he was not going to tell Coltrane that he too was to be one of the escort. He reasoned that had he done so there would have been no way of freeing himself from the man's attention for the remainder of the night. He bought Coltrane the obligatory beer, finished his own and managed to slip out of the saloon without Coltrane seeing him.

2

'Just the man I wanted to see,' said Captain John Fisher when he met Cobb outside the assay office the following morning. 'Want to earn a few extra dollars?'

I'm always open to suggestions,' said Cobb. 'What man isn't?'

'I want you to stand guard in the office when they start bringing in their gold,' said Fisher. 'My regular guard got himself involved in a brawl last night and he's in no fit state to do anything at the moment. He managed to get himself a broken leg and a broken arm. It also means that one of you will have to drive the wagon to Geraldine. He was the driver.'

'His bad luck is my good luck,' said Cobb. 'I'm not so sure about driving the wagon though, but if that's the way it has to be, so be it. I reckon we can manage. OK, when do I start?'

'It's a bit early, but you might as well start right now although there won't be anything for you to do for a while,' said Fisher. 'You'll need your pistol and your rifle. The sight of a rifle tends to put off any trouble-makers, especially if the man holding it looks as though he can use it.'

'I'll go and get them,' said Cobb. 'Oh, just one thing: how much?'

'I can't afford to pay you a lot, two dollars a day, that's all,' said Fisher. 'Still, two dollars a day is better than nothing.'

'Like you say, it's better than nothing,' agreed Cobb. 'Do you get many troublemakers?'

'Not many,' said Fisher, 'but there's always the odd miner who thinks the price we're giving him is not enough, or he's convinced that the scales are tipped in our favour. That's the usual complaint. Most of them are quite certain that their gold weighs at least an ounce more than it actually does.

There's always the odd one who tries to slip some fool's gold in to make up the weight as well. I'm up to all their tricks though. After three years in this business you soon get to know all the dodges. Some of them even try to pass sand off as gold dust.'

'OK, I guess I can deal with that,' said Cobb. 'Mind you, don't expect me to know the difference between fool's gold and real gold. I know fool's gold is iron pyrites but I can never tell which is which. As far as I'm concerned that's your business, not mine. I'll just go and collect my guns. I'll be back in ten minutes.'

Ten minutes later, Cobb took up his position in the assay office wondering why he had been asked to start so early. There was no sign of any miners and there was nothing for him to do other than sit and wait. However, much to his surprise, the miners started to drift into town later that afternoon.

'There's always one or two who come in early,' said Fisher. 'They seem to have this idea that they're going to get a better price that way. They'll really start coming in tomorrow.'

'Did you manage to get all your guards for the escort?' asked Cobb. 'I see the notice has been taken down.'

'Five of you,' said Fisher. 'One of the others looks like the side of a barn. He says he can use a gun and he certainly looks mean enough.'

'Sam Coltrane,' said Cobb.

'You know him then?' said Fisher. 'I certainly wouldn't like to tangle with him in a fist fight, that's for sure.'

'It would be rather like trying to knock down a three-foot thick brick wall with the flat of your hand,' agreed Cobb. 'Yes, I know him. I'm surprised you don't. I hear he's quite a character around town.'

'I've heard about him and I've seen him around,' said Fisher. 'I've heard how he gets his drink as well. I'm not a drinking man though, in fact I don't think I've ever been inside the saloon. He's a big man sure enough, but I don't think he's very bright. He'll do his job and be no bother. The other three are nothing special. I think they're like you, just drifting through. Two of them know each other and that's something I'd rather not have. I prefer it when nobody knows anybody else, there's less likelihood that they're planning to steal the gold. With you around though, I feel it's quite safe.'

'I know Sam Coltrane,' Cobb pointed out.

'I'd hardly call having a man bum a couple of drinks off you as knowing him,' said Fisher. 'The third man is a very quiet one, it's hard to know what to make of him. He claims to have been in the army as well. A corporal he reckons. In fact I've told all of them to be here at four o'clock so's they can get to know who they're travelling with.'

Six miners came into the office during the course of the day and, as predicted, all but one seemed convinced that their gold weighed more than the scales indicated. Although they grumbled, they took their money and immediately headed for either the saloon or the hotel. At four o'clock, Sam Coltrane and three other men arrived.

'Sam Coltrane you already know, Major,' said Fisher. 'This is Tom Williams, an ex-corporal, Ed Bishop and Jack Crane. Gentlemen, this is Major Cobb, he'll be in command of the party.'

'Major!' grunted Tom Williams. 'I had kind of hoped I'd got away from the army.'

'I'm not in the army any longer,' said Cobb.

'Good; don't expect me to treat you like I would an officer when I was a soldier,' said Williams.

'I won't,' said Cobb. 'But just remember who's in charge, that's all.'

'Same applies to us,' said Ed Bishop. 'We signed up to do a job, that's all. We don't take no orders off nobody.'

'Just do your job and we'll get along fine,' said Cobb.

'You never said you were in on this,' said Sam Coltrane. 'Fine by me though. You never said you was a major either. I tried to join the army once but for some reason they turned me down. I reckon it was 'cos I was too big for their uniforms but they never said.'

'Probably that was it,' said Cobb. 'OK, now we all know who we are, I'll see you all here at six on Monday morning. In the meantime don't get yourselves into any trouble, don't turn up here drunk on Monday and don't talk to anyone about what you are doing.'

'Yes, sir!' said Tom Williams, standing to attention and saluting sarcastically. 'Everybody knows exactly what we're doin', it sure ain't no secret. Still, once an officer, always an officer I suppose.' He turned and left the office. '0-six hundred hours it is, sir!' he called back.

The other two sneered at Cobb as they left the office, leaving Sam Coltrane. Coltrane watched them disappear and then waited around, obviously there was something on his mind.

'What is it, Sam?' asked Cobb.

'Well I ain't sure,' said Sam. 'It's just that I reckon I've seen the one called Jack Crane somewheres before. First time I've ever seen him in this town that's for sure, but I seen his face, I know I have. I might forget names an' I've never had no schoolin' so I can't read an' write, but I never forget a face. The name Jack Crane don't mean much either. I'm sure that face didn't go with that name when I saw him before.'

'And where would that be?' asked Fisher.

'That's just it, I can't remember,' said Sam. 'I ain't been to Geraldine in more'n two years, so I don't reckon it was there. That leaves either Kingsville or Turkey Bend. They're both about four days from here. I was in Kingsville about six months ago an' Turkey Bend about six weeks ago. Most likely it was Turkey Bend. Darned if I can remember why I should've remembered the face though. I'll have to think about it.'

'He was probably talking just for the sake of it,' said Fisher, when Sam had left. 'As far as I know both Jack Crane and Ed Bishop are clean. I make a point of checking wanted posters in the sheriff's office, I even checked on you and there's no posters out on any of you.'

'Thanks for the vote of confidence,' said Cobb with a dry laugh. 'Still, I suppose you have to check what you can. I must admit that I have some misgivings about those two though. I consider myself a good judge of a man and those two don't exactly instil confidence. I'll talk to Sam later; he might have remembered something by then.'

'If there is anything to remember. OK, I'll leave it to you,' said Fisher. 'Now, you said something about not having anywhere to sleep for the next day or two. Have you found anywhere? I don't hold out much chance of you getting in at the rooming-house, I hear it's already fully booked. The miners who arrived early have booked their friends in.'

'Not yet,' said Cobb. 'I haven't had chance to talk to Mary at the hotel but I don't hold out much hope.'

'Then you can bed down here,' said Fisher. 'You'll have to sleep on the floor, but it's better than nowhere and it'll be free.'

'Where are you sleeping?' asked Cobb. 'You're not in the hotel, I know that. I'm the only guest there at the moment.'

'I always room with Sheriff McGovan,' said Fisher. 'We used to be in the army together. He was my platoon sergeant for a long time. We both left about the same time.'

At six o'clock, Fisher closed the office and Cobb returned to the hotel where he discovered that two women had already established themselves. It seemed that during the course of the evening more miners had drifted into town in readiness for the following day and these two farmers' wives were starting early. Cobb decided that he might as well spend the night in a comfortable bed, since it would probably be the last occasion he could do so for some time.

Mary somewhat grudgingly supplied him with a meal that evening when she made it quite plain that she expected him to vacate his room early the following morning. After he had eaten he went along to the saloon where, as expected, he was accosted by Sam Coltrane.

'Have you remembered where you saw Jack Crane?' asked Cobb, as he paid for beers for both himself and Coltrane.

'Naw,' admitted Coltrane. 'I been thinkin' about that ever since I left you. I even followed them both down to the roomin'-house, but I still can't think where or when it was. I have seen him before, I know that. I never forget a face. Don't you worry none, it'll come to me sometime.'

'I wasn't worrying,' said Cobb. 'I think I'll go and see the sheriff. It could be that he knows them, but I doubt it.'

Suddenly Coltrane slapped the counter with the flat of his hand. 'That's it!' he said loudly, making heads turn to look at them. Cobb placed a restraining hand on Coltrane's arm. 'You sayin' you was goin' to see the sheriff reminded me,' Coltrane continued, lowering his voice. 'It *was* in Turkey Bend I saw him. I thought it was. Yeh, I remember now.'

'OK, so you saw him in Turkey Bend,' said Cobb. 'What makes you so sure?'

'The prison,' said Coltrane. 'Yeh, the prison. Oh, I forgot, you probably don't know. There's a prison just outside Turkey Bend an' I was there — in Turkey Bend, not the prison, I ain't never been inside a jail, let alone a prison — when Crane was released from the prison. I didn't know who he was or where he'd come from at the time. All I can remember is him sayin' he couldn't afford to buy me drink on

37

account of he'd just been released. His name wasn't Jack Crane then though, I'm sure of that. I think somebody knew him an' called him somethin' else. It sure wasn't Crane. Don't worry, I'll remember what he called himself.'

'Keep thinking,' said Cobb. 'I'll go and see the sheriff. In the meantime you keep this to yourself. You don't even mention it to Captain Fisher. Do you understand?'

'Yes, sir, Major, sir,' said Coltrane. He drained his glass and looked meaningfully at Cobb. Cobb relented and bought him another beer.

'Captain Fisher has already checked on all of you,' said Sheriff McGovan, taking a handful of wanted posters from a drawer and handing them to Cobb. 'There's nothing there, I can assure you, but you can take a look for yourself if it'll ease your mind. I can't see why you're so bothered though, it's just three days' work for you, isn't it? Mind, it's nice to see a man taking his work so seriously.'

'Three days or three years,' said Cobb. 'I like to have things right. If anything goes wrong it'll be my life on the line and not yours, Sheriff.'

Cobb studied the posters but, as the sheriff had said, there were none which could have been Jack Crane, Ed Bishop or Tom Williams. Eventually he put the posters to one side and sighed.

'I told you there was nothing,' said McGovan. 'Had there been Captain Fisher would never have hired them.'

'It is my belief that this Jack Crane, or whatever he calls himself,' said Cobb, 'has recently been released from prison. The prison at Turkey Bend. That means that there wouldn't be any flyers out on him. Do you keep old posters?'

'Nope,' said the sheriff. 'If I did that this room would be full. I get rid of them as soon as I'm notified they've been caught.'

'Is there any way of finding out who was released from prison, say about six weeks ago?' asked Cobb.

'It can be done,' said the sheriff, 'but

it'll take some time. Mind you, if he's using a different name now it'll be almost impossible. We often get the ex-prisoners through here and I reckon most of them have changed their name. There's nothing unusual in that and there's certainly no law against it. A man can call himself what the hell he likes if he wants to.'

'I thought that might be the case,' said Cobb. 'I wouldn't bother checking; I'm pretty certain that he wasn't calling himself Jack Crane then.'

'You've been listening to Sam Coltrane,' said the sheriff with a wry smile. 'Captain Fisher told me that he'd been sounding off about having seen Crane somewhere else. Major, I'll give you a piece of advice: whatever Sam Coltrane says I'd take with a large pinch of salt. He once claimed to have witnessed a murder. Quite certain of it he was, but the man who was supposed to have been murdered turned up two days later. We never did find another body either. Sam has these wild ideas sometimes. I think he does it just to be the centre of attraction. I've no idea where he came from or who his parents were, but I do know he's a bit simple in the head — except when it comes to bummin' drinks off folk like you.'

'Maybe you're right,' admitted Cobb. 'OK, Sheriff, sorry to have wasted your time. It's just that I like to have things right. That's the result of all those years in the army I suppose. You ought to know that though. I hear you were a sergeant serving with Captain Fisher.'

'Twelve years,' said the sheriff. 'I sometimes wish I'd stayed in. Life was a whole lot easier.'

'I know exactly what you mean,' said Cobb.

He returned to the saloon, which was by then very crowded. He eventually located Sam Coltrane, but Sam still could not remember what name Jack Crane had used in Turkey Bend. Unlike the sheriff, Cobb was quite convinced that Sam was telling the truth.

He also realized that he was probably

being rather too cautious. Even if Sam Coltrane was correct and Crane had recently been released from prison, what could be more natural than for such a man to try and earn himself a few dollars? However, he still had a very uneasy feeling about both Jack Crane and Ed Bishop. In fact, he was beginning to have doubts about the whole thing.

Although Cobb had elected to spend that night in the comfort of a bed, there were occasions during the night when he wondered if he had done the right thing. There seemed to be a continual procession of men up and down the stairs for most of the night and it was not until the early hours that the noise abated. True to her word, a very bleary-eyed Mary served him breakfast of ham and eggs and reminded him to get his things out of the room. As he was leaving the hotel he met eight more women and already they had several men in tow.

He looked at them as they went

inside and wondered exactly what made seemingly normal women go in for such a business. More importantly, he thought, what kind of man would allow his wife to do it or, as he was given to understand, force his wife into such a business. He sighed and shook his head. The answer was quite simple — money.

It was simply an extension of something he had often witnessed when he had been in the army leading a patrol of men. They had often camped the night in farmers' barns and for a mere two dollars a time, the farmer's wife had taken on his entire platoon. In most cases it had been the farmer who had stood at the door taking the money.

By the time he reached the assay office there was already a long queue of miners waiting to sell their gold. Captain Fisher arrived at the same moment as Cobb. Sheriff McGovan also took up a position outside the office.

'Most of them will be through today,'

explained Fisher. 'There'll be a few in on Saturday and probably one or two, who pan the rivers up in the Yuma Mountains, on Sunday. We used to close up on Sunday but they complained they couldn't get here on time so I agreed to extend it. Strangely enough, the Yuma Mountain prospectors usually bring in more gold per man than the Yuma Valley crowd.'

The day passed slowly as far as Cobb was concerned. There was little for him to do which had the effect of making time drag. There were a couple of minor disagreements, but nothing which required his serious attention and certainly did not involve the use of guns or any other physical force. Sheriff McGovan swiftly dealt with such cases.

From where he was, Cobb could see that the barber was doing a good, steady trade even at his inflated prices. The general store also appeared to be well serviced as the miners stocked up on supplies to see them through until the following month. It was also very noticeable that, unlike the women from the outlying farms, the women from the town were conspicuous by their absence. Even the menfolk appeared to be doing whatever business was necessary and then returning to their homes. Cobb wondered if this was to make certain that their women did not try to earn a few extra dollars.

Apart from the sheriff and his deputy, the storekeepers, the hotel and the saloon, the only other citizens of note to be out on the street were the preacher and two rather large and very severe-looking women.

The preacher had taken up position outside the hotel, flanked by his formidable duo and spent almost the entire day pronouncing on the sins of the flesh, the evils of gambling and urging the miners to contribute towards the upkeep of the church. He also told the farm women that they were inviting the wrath of God upon themselves, their husbands and their farms.

Cobb did not see anyone actually put

gold or money into the metal buckets the women were continually shoving in front of the miners. However, he was more than surprised when, just as the assay office was about to close, the preacher came into the office, weighed in some gold and left clutching almost $200. Obviously his time had not been completely fruitless.

When the office closed, Captain Fisher, Cobb and the sheriff took the gold and what money was left along to the bank where it was safely locked away. Fisher handed Cobb a key to the office.

'I'll be back at seven in the morning,' said Fisher. 'You won't get any bother, everyone knows we don't keep the gold or money overnight. Here's your two dollars for today. You'll probably need it.'

Cobb decided that he was not going to risk the food on offer at the eating-house, but it seemed that the miners did not share his inhibitions. The place was full. The only other place where food was available was the bakery. He bought a small loaf, some cheese, two pickled eggs and something the baker claimed to be a mustard pickle. The first taste of the pickle was enough for Cobb and he settled for bread and cheese and the eggs which he ate in the relative comfort of the office.

After he had eaten, he went along to the saloon where he was quite surprised to discover that the prices had not been inflated. He ordered a beer and looked about for Sam Coltrane. Sam acknowledged him but did not try to bum a beer from him. He was plainly doing very well and did not need Cobb. Cobb also noted that there were at least four farmers' women doing a steady trade between the bar and some small rooms at the rear.

After a short time, Tom Williams, the ex-corporal, joined Cobb at the bar. Both men drank in silence for some time before Williams eventually spoke.

'Don't it strike you as kind of funny?' asked Williams.

'Does what strike me as funny?' asked Cobb.

'This whole setup about escortin' the gold to Geraldine,' said Williams. 'No, sir, it just don't make sense to me. I mean, there must be a hell of a lot of gold an' it just don't make sense for it to be entrusted to five complete strangers.'

'Captain Fisher says that the system works,' said Cobb. 'I suppose he knows his business.'

'Would you do it?' asked Williams.

'I don't have to,' said Cobb.

'No, sir, you don't,' said Williams, 'and neither does Fisher. There's somethin' about this whole thing what don't sit right with me and I sure as hell wouldn't trust Bishop an' Crane with a bar of candy, let alone all that gold.'

'You can always back out,' said Cobb. 'We can probably find someone else, or manage with just the four of us.'

'Major,' said Williams, 'I don't know quite how you figure in all this, but I do know you don't work for Fisher or the state. Sam Coltrane told me you were a stranger in town. I think that like me, you need the money. Ten dollars a day for three days ain't somethin' I can turn my nose up at, especially since I was goin' to Geraldine anyhow. No, I'll stick with it, but that don't mean I have to like it. Think about it, Major, by the time we leave on Monday I reckon there'll be more'n twenty thousand dollars in gold, maybe even a whole lot more. That could work out at least four thousand apiece. No, I ask you, where the hell could the likes of you an' me get that kind of money?'

'Are you suggesting that we steal it?' asked Cobb.

'It's a thought,' said Williams, 'an' any other man might think seriously about it. In fact, I wouldn't be surprised if Bishop an' Crane aren't workin' out how to get their hands on it right now.'

'What about Sam Coltrane?' asked Cobb.

'Naw,' said Williams with a wry

49

laugh. 'He might be as thick as they come, but I don't think he's a dishonest man. Apart from you an' me, he's the only one we can rely on.'

'And what makes you think you can rely on me?' asked Cobb.

'Just a feelin', Major,' replied Williams, 'just a feelin'. Don't worry, I ain't in the business of stealin' gold or anythin' else. I'll do my job, take the thirty dollars an' be glad of it. It's just that I thought you ought to know that it don't sit right with me, that's all.'

'Your feelings are noted, Corporal,' said Cobb.

3

Tom Williams had been correct; there was something not quite right with the whole thing and the more he thought about it, the more Cobb worried. He resolved to try and clarify the situation the following morning. The result of his worrying was that he spent a rather restless night.

'Captain,' he said to Fisher when he arrived at the assay office, 'I suppose you know your own business, but there's something which doesn't seem right about this as far as I'm concerned.'

'Major,' said Fisher, 'I know exactly what you are going to say. Why should I entrust all that gold with complete strangers? You are quite right when you say I know my own business, so just take it from me that it works. Even if you did steal the gold, which is quite possible, I agree, how far do you think you would get? Believe me, there'd be more law enforcement officers and more soldiers on your tail than you could count in next to no time. I'll admit that all that gold apparently just for the taking must be one hell of a temptation to a lot of people and there are probably some who believe they could get away with it. If that's what you're thinking, be my guest, try it. There isn't a state or territory in the country in which you could hide. You've been in the army, you must know how they work, and you probably know quite a bit about law enforcement officers as well.'

'Yes, I know,' agreed Cobb, 'but as you rightly say, there are those who might think they could get away with it. Remember there's a lot of wilderness out there. A man could hide up for years and not be found.'

'I agree,' said Fisher, 'but what man in his right mind would want to spend all that time out there sitting on a heap of gold he can't use? Human nature being what it is, the idea of stealing the gold would be to spend it. That's the way things are, believe me.'

'You seem to have all the angles sorted out,' admitted Cobb. 'OK, Captain, I'll go along with it.'

'I thought you would,' said Fisher. 'Don't worry, my people at Geraldine will be sent a wire the moment you leave here. They know how long it takes and if for some reason you are late they'll be sending out someone to look for you.'

Despite Captain Fisher's assurances, Cobb was still not really convinced and neither was Tom Williams when he met him that evening in the saloon. However, both men agreed to go along with it since they both needed the money they were being paid.

★   ★   ★

At six o'clock precisely on the Monday morning, all five men gathered in front of the assay office. The gold was loaded on to the wagon and Cobb marvelled at just how little space it took. There were four boxes about eighteen inches square by about eight or nine inches in depth and although they were good and strong it was obvious that a determined man would soon have them open.

Ed Bishop and Jack Crane set themselves slightly apart from the other three, an action which Cobb found slightly odd, but he had to assume that they were simply not the sociable types and did not question them. Captain Fisher had also provided enough food and water for the three days and at 6.15 Cobb led his charges out of town.

It was very noticeable that Bishop and Crane kept themselves apart from the others, choosing to ride at the rear of the wagon. The wagon itself was driven by Sam Coltrane, who claimed to be an expert in the art of wagon driving. His horse was tethered behind. Cobb had to admit that Sam appeared to know what he was doing. Tom

Williams took up position alongside the horse pulling the wagon whilst Cobb rode alongside the wagon.

If Cobb and Williams had expected any trouble, it certainly did not materialize on that day and they eventually made camp just before sunset amongst a clump of thorn trees. Their meal consisted of salt pork, beans and turnips which Sam Coltrane insisted on cooking. Once again, Coltrane surprised Cobb in producing quite an edible meal. There was obviously a lot more to this seemingly simple man-mountain than at first appeared. Cobb could not help but wonder how he would react if they were attacked.

They set off again shortly after dawn the following morning. The sky was unusually overcast and the threat of rain lay ahead of them. For some strange reason Cobb had a sense of unease and ordered Tom Williams to ride on ahead in an attempt to forestall any surprise attack. After about half an hour Williams returned.

'Two men ridin' this way,' he said. 'They don't seem to be makin' any attempt to hide. They're probably just travellin' through.'

'Very likely,' agreed Cobb. 'Be ready though, just in case.' He passed the same warning on to Bishop and Crane who simply smirked and nodded.

Eventually two riders could be seen, obviously not in any hurry and heading towards them. They appeared innocent enough but Cobb still had the sense of unease he had felt earlier.

They eventually met up with the two riders who both stopped and lounged forward in their saddles.

'Looks like it's goin' to rain,' observed one of the men. 'Goin' far?'

'Geraldine,' replied Cobb. 'And you?'

'Nowheres in particular,' replied one of the men. 'In fact I reckon we've come about as far as we need to.'

'Meaning what?' asked Cobb.

'Meaning that we came for the gold you're carryin',' replied the man.

Both men were faster than either Cobb or Williams on the draw and even if they had not been, the fact that Bishop and Crane had now drawn their guns and had them pointed at them would have made any resistance futile. Cobb simply gave a wry smile, nodded and spoke to Crane.

'I might have guessed you'd have someone else,' he said. 'I had the feeling that you were going to try something.'

'That's right, Major,' said Crane. 'Meet my partners. Now, you can do this the easy way, or we can kill you all. Coltrane, get off that wagon.' Sam Coltrane looked at Cobb who nodded.

'And how far do you think you are going to get?' Cobb asked.

'Far enough,' said Crane. 'That's somethin' you ain't got to worry about, Major. Now, off your horses, throw your guns over here and don't even think about trying to kill us. None of us are wanted for murder and we'd hate for you to be the reason we are. We're takin' the gold.'

'OK, be my guest,' said Cobb. 'It doesn't belong to us so why should we worry about it? It won't take long for the army or the law to come on out after you.'

'First they've got to find out we've taken it,' said Bishop.

'Without the wagon it won't take us long to ride into Geraldine,' said Cobb.

'Ride!' said Bishop with a dry laugh. 'Who said anythin' about you ridin' anywhere? I don't think you get the idea, Major. We take the wagon, your guns and your horses. From here on you walk to Geraldine.'

'I see,' said Cobb. 'OK, you seem to have it all worked out, but I still don't think much of your chances of getting away with it.'

'That's for us to worry about,' said Crane. 'All you've got to worry about is will your boot leather last out. Now, off your horses, throw your guns over here and I'll even let you start walking now.'

Cobb sighed and nodded to Williams and Coltrane while he too dismounted.

'What about food?' he asked. 'You wouldn't expect a man to walk that far without food and water, would you?'

'Major,' said Crane with a laugh and looking up at the sky. 'It looks to me like water is goin' to be the least of your problems. As for food, they tell me lizard an' rattlesnake don't taste too bad an' there's plenty of both in these parts.'

There was nothing the three of them could do. As far as Cobb was concerned there was nothing to be gained by attempting to stop them. Their lives were far more important than the gold. A few minutes later, now with four horses in tow, their three and the one belonging to the man who now drove the wagon, the riders were heading east. Cobb made a mental note of their direction.

'I ain't at all surprised,' said Williams, as he watched them slowly head away. 'I said I didn't trust them or the way Fisher handled it. I don't know about you, Major, but I reckon that Captain

John Fisher is part of all this.'

'Me too,' said Sam Coltrane. 'I never said anythin' but I saw those two, Sheriff McGovan an' Fisher talkin'. I don't think they saw me, or if they did they probably thought I was too drunk to notice. Drunk I might've been, but I ain't never been too drunk to know what's goin' on.'

'Then why the hell didn't you say somethin'?' demanded Williams.

'Like what?' asked Sam. 'Ain't no law what says a man can't talk to who the hell he wants to, is there?'

'Sam's right,' said Cobb. 'He might have told me and I might have tackled Fisher or the sheriff about it. They could easily have made up some story.'

'OK,' said Williams. 'I guess we can all be wiser men after the event. I reckon we'd better start walkin'.'

'You walk to Geraldine if you want to,' Sam suddenly said. 'That's just what they want us to do. They can't travel too fast with that wagon, 'specially goin' the way they went.

That's pretty rough country up there an' they'll soon find out that somethin' like a wagon is goin' to hold 'em back.'

'Are you sure?' asked Cobb. 'It seems to me that if we follow them we are heading into country where there's hardly a living thing. At least if we keep on towards Geraldine we might be met by somebody or even come across a few farms. We'd be better off that way.'

'You do what you've a mind to, Major,' said Sam. 'I was born an' raised up in them hills, I know 'em like the back of my hand. I'm goin' out to get my horse an' guns back. They're the only things I own an' I ain't goin' to stand by an' let some stupid outlaws leave my horse to die somewheres.'

'Die?' queried Williams.

'Sure,' said Sam. 'A horse out there alone is easy meat for a mountain lion an' there's plenty of them up there. This time of year they'll have young as well an' no mountain lion is goin' to bother with rabbits or deer when there's a load of good eatin' right there on the hoof.'

'And just how far do you think they'll get before they have to abandon the wagon?' asked Cobb.

Sam glanced towards the hills and smiled. 'Looks like it's already started to rain up there,' he said. 'They'll have to cross Mitre Creek an' that could be a real problem. Normally it ain't too bad, but it don't take that much rain for the creek to fill up an' when it does it's almost impossible to get across. They'll never be able to get the wagon over, that's for sure.'

'OK,' said Cobb, 'just supposing we go along with what you say, how far is it to this creek?'

'If we start walkin' now we ought to reach it by this time tomorrow,' said Sam. 'If it has started rainin' up there — an' it sure looks like it to me — even if they reached it tonight, they'll never be able to cross it.'

'You know,' said Tom Williams, 'you ain't as dumb as you look. Sure, I'll go along with what you say. They reach this Mitre Creek, find they can't get the wagon across so they have to transfer the gold to their horses. You saw it all boxed up, Major, was it in bags or loose?'

'In bags,' said Cobb. 'I'd say about half a pound each.'

'OK, so they'll bust open the boxes,' said Williams. 'Bags that size will fit easy enough in their saddle-bags an' they'll leave the wagon. The chances are they'll also leave our horses as well. The guns they'll probably take with 'em, but we can't hope for too much. Yes, Major, I'm with Sam. We follow them.'

'If for no other reason than to get my horse back, I agree,' said Cobb. 'We get them back and then ride like hell for Geraldine to alert the authorities.'

'I'm with you on that,' said Williams. 'I sure ain't goin' to get myself killed on account of some gold I don't own.'

'They might not pay us,' said Cobb. 'We were supposed to deliver that gold to get paid. They could say we failed and refuse to pay us.'

'Then none of us will be any worse off,' said Williams.

'We'll be without our guns,' reminded Cobb.

'Just one of those things, Major,' said Williams. 'Well, I suppose we'd better start walkin' right now if we want to find our horses.'

'Since you know those hills, you lead the way,' Cobb said to Sam.

'Yes, sir, Major, sir,' beamed Sam, obviously enjoying the experience of being in charge for one of the few times in his life.

Although it became increasingly obvious that it was now raining quite heavily higher up in the hills, luck was with them and whilst it became quite windy, the rain held off. At dusk Sam led them to a large, deep overhang of rock alongside which there was a fairly large pool of clear water. They wasted no time in gathering dry grass and wood with which to make a fire and then Sam appeared to perform a miracle. He scrabbled about at the back of the overhang and suddenly shouted with triumph. He held up a line and hook.

'Me an' my brother used to use this place when we was kids,' he announced. 'This pool has some of the best catfish in the state. Good eatin' is catfish an' they is the easiest things in the world to catch. I remembered we buried a line just in case we should ever get caught out here. Never did of course, but we kept the line here all the same.'

'There's just one problem as far as I can see,' said Cobb. 'To catch fish, you need bait. Now look as hard as I might, I can't see anything we could use as bait, not even a dried out bird.'

'Don't need no proper bait,' said Sam, laughing. 'I told you, catfish is the dumbest, easiest things in the world to catch. Stupid they are, they're just too nosy for their own good. That's why they is so darned easy to catch. You just watch.'

He tore a strip of material from a red

neckerchief he was wearing, wrapped it round the rusting hook on the line and then, holding one end of the line, threw the rest of it as far out into the pool as he could. He then slowly hauled the line back. He seemed quite disappointed when nothing had taken the lure the first time. However, his second cast was very successful and a few minutes later he had a black catfish beached. He gave it a sharp blow on its head which appeared to kill it and then cast the line again. Moments later he was hauling in a fish twice the size of the first.

'These two ought to be enough,' he said. 'OK, one of you gut 'em an' I'll mix up some clay.'

'Mix some clay?' asked Williams. 'What the hell for?'

'Easy to see you ain't no country boy,' said Sam, with a wry laugh. 'I might not be able to read an' write but I can sure as hell find somethin' to eat even out in the driest desert. We cover the fish in clay, stick 'em on the fire for about half an hour an' then you've got cooked fish. Real tasty done that way, keeps all the flavour in. You break off the clay an' all the skin an' spines comes off with it.'

'I'll take your word for it,' muttered Williams.

True to his word, half an hour later they were picking gingerly at steaming hot fish and even Cobb, who normally did not like fish, had to admit that it tasted very good.

'I'm glad we brought you along,' said Cobb, after they had eaten. 'You are full of surprises aren't you, Sam? What made you move into town?'

'Work,' said Sam. 'Out here might be a great place for a kid growin' up, but folk don't stay kids forever. My brother was the first to go, somewhere in Texas the last I heard of him. Then my ma an' pa died so there was nothin' to keep me out here. We had a bit of a farm about five miles from here. I come out sometimes to tend their graves an' think. Only trouble is I ain't too good at thinkin'. The old place is a ruin now, only a couple of walls left. Never was much good as a farm anyhow. Why my folks stayed I'll never know.'

'Why didn't you lead us there?' asked Williams.

'I know thinkin' ain't my strong point,' said Sam, 'but even I get the occasional idea. I figured that maybe them outlaws found it and stayed there the night. Since we ain't got the guns to tackle 'em, it didn't seem such a good idea, even to me.'

'You ought to try thinking more often,' said Cobb. 'You might even become quite good at it. How much further to this Mitre Creek?'

'I already told you,' said Sam. 'We should reach it by midday tomorrow, providin' the rain holds off that is.'

Unfortunately, during the night the rain did come and, although they were able to keep dry under the overhang, the scene which greeted them the following morning was one of a sea of mud as far as the eye could see. The pool from which Sam had caught the catfish was now twice its original size and appeared to be increasing by the minute as water drained off the surrounding land.

At first it was obvious that trying to negotiate the mud and the rain would be a waste of time and Cobb decided that they would be better off waiting for the rain to stop. He reasoned that wherever Crane and Bishop were at that moment, it was quite likely that they too were in the same predicament. It was quite certain, as far as Cobb was concerned, that attempting to drive the wagon through the muddy ground would be almost impossible. Eventually, just before midday, the rain ceased, the sun shone and they started on their way, once again led by Sam Coltrane.

The delay obviously meant that they would not reach Mitre Creek until late that evening, if then, and the only consolation was that Crane and Bishop would also be slowed down.

Sam had said that his old homestead

was about five miles from where they had spent the night. Such a journey, even walking, should normally have taken two hours at the most. As it was, the ground being as wet as it was, it took them almost four hours.

'Maybe this wasn't such a good idea after all,' said Cobb.

'That's the worst of it over with,' said Sam. 'From here on up to Mitre Creek the ground is more rocky than anythin' else. Difficult for a wagon but easy for a horse an' walkin'.'

'It looks like the rain has passed over,' said Williams, looking up at the now cloudless sky. 'Let's hope it stays that way.'

'Should do,' said Sam. 'In these parts at this time of year the rain comes suddenly an' goes just as sudden. Anyhow — ' he swept his arm in an arc — 'this is where I was born an' raised. not much is it? Ma and Pa are buried just up that hill. Mind if I go an' tidy things up a bit? Looks like I was right about them spendin' the night here though.' He pointed at the remains of a fire.

'Personally,' said Cobb, 'I'm all for staying here for the night. It's only about three hours until sunset and the ground is drying out quite quickly. I suggest we get ourselves a good night's sleep and start out early in the morning.'

'I'm with you,' said Williams. 'I don't suppose you can find us more food, Sam? Maybe we should have caught a few more catfish.'

'Ain't no catfish round here,' said Sam. 'There might be a few deer an' plenty of rabbits out in the hills but not much else 'ceptin' a few lizards, rattlers an' mountain lions. I guess we'll just have to go hungry. See if you can find some wood what ain't too wet. We're goin' to need a fire tonight. It gets mighty cold sometimes an' since we ain't got no blankets we got to have somethin' to keep us warm.'

Finding dry wood was quite impossible although Tom Williams did manage to get a fire started using some dry grass which had somehow escaped the rain by being sheltered against one of the old walls. It was touch and go for quite some time as the flames threatened to die out. However, after all three of them searching everywhere they could think of, they did manage to gather enough dry grass and a very small quantity of brushwood. Armed with these meagre pickings, they did eventually create a fire on which all but the wettest of wood caught light. They piled up more wood close to the fire in an attempt to dry it out.

Wet wood and flames create a lot of smoke and at first Cobb gazed up at the steady, thick plume and worried that it might be seen by the four outlaws. Sam obviously knew what he was thinking.

'Ain't nothin' we can do about it,' he said. 'You've got the choice; risk bein' seen by the smoke, or freeze to death durin' the night. I reckon they'll be too far ahead to see it.'

'You are probably right,' admitted

Cobb. 'OK, I suppose it's far better to wake up in the morning than freeze to death.'

'I got to thinkin' about food,' said Sam. 'Have you ever tried rattler?' Tom Williams shook his head.

'I did once,' said Cobb. 'I can't say that I enjoyed it. Why?'

'Well, I said I could find food even in the desert,' said Sam. 'I still reckon I could if I had to. Anyhow, me an' my brother caught a rattler once an' cooked it just to see what it tasted like. It warn't that bad if I remember right.'

'I'm prepared to try anything,' said Williams. 'But where do you find rattlers in this wet ground?'

'See the top of that small hill . . . ?' Sam pointed behind the farm ruins. 'Well, when we was kids there was always a lot of rattlers up there. They was never no trouble, they never are if you leave 'em alone. Anyhow, as I say, there was always a few rattlers up there an' I reckon there probably still is. They is easy enough to find if you know

73

where to look. What say we try to catch us a couple?'

'What with?' asked Tom Williams. 'I sure don't fancy tryin' to catch one with my bare hands.'

'Easy enough,' said Sam. 'We break off a couple of thin branches with a fork at one end an' use 'em to trap the rattlers behind the head.'

'It sounds too easy to me,' said Williams.

'I've seen it done,' said Cobb. 'OK, I'll give it a try.'

A short time later, they were at the top of the hill without a rattlesnake in sight, Sam did not seem bothered and proceeded to turn over some large stones. At first he found nothing but then suddenly let out a shout as he lunged with his stick. The other two ran forward to see a large rattlesnake trapped under the fork of the stick. It writhed and twisted for a while as Sam seemed keen to show off his prize. He eventually ended the snake's life by stamping on its head.

Cobb tried his hand at catching another snake he found under a rock and was very lucky in that he narrowly avoided being bitten. Sam then attacked the snake and soon had it pinned down.

Cooking the snakes on this occasion, unlike cooking the catfish, meant simply throwing the bodies into the fire and eventually dragging them out. Although badly charred, they did not taste too bad. At least it was food.

4

They started out for Mitre Creek as soon as first light broke. Although still quite wet underfoot, the ground had dried out sufficiently enough to give them a fairly firm footing. Sam Coltrane assured them that it would not take very long to reach their destination. Cobb's one thought and hope was that they were not making a wasted journey.

As Sam had predicted, it did not take them that long to reach the creek, just over three hours and it appeared that luck was with them. From the cover of some rocks, they looked down on the now swollen waters of the creek. There was no sign of Jack Crane, Ed Bishop, or the other two men, but the horses belonging to Cobb, Williams and Coltrane and the wagon were standing on a piece of high ground which was almost surrounded by swirling water. The only way to reach them was across a narrow spit of land about ten feet wide.

At first Cobb wondered why the horses had remained, but closer inspection showed that they were all tethered to the wagon. Tom Williams volunteered to climb to the top of another hill just in case the outlaws were still in the area. With no guns with which to defend themselves, it was vital that they were not seen. He returned some time later saying that there was no sign of them.

As expected, the boxes which had contained the gold had been broken open and were now empty. Once again, Sam Coltrane surprised both Cobb and Williams when he suddenly whooped with delight and produced a pistol from his saddle-bag.

'At least we got one gun!' said Coltrane, obviously very pleased with himself. 'It's an old DeBrame what belonged to my pa. It's only a five shot, but there's a box of bullets for it here as well, about twenty rounds. Still, it'll get us out of trouble I reckon.'

'Unfortunately they seem to have taken the others,' said Cobb. 'I wonder why they didn't take that one?'

'That's easy,' said Sam, with a laugh. 'They didn't look. OK, Major, we got our horses an' the wagon an' we got one gun. What do we do now?'

'Leave the wagon here and head for Geraldine,' said Cobb.

'What about the gold?' asked Sam. 'You just goin' to let 'em get away with it?'

'It don't belong to us,' said Tom Williams. 'I for one ain't bothered about playin' nursemaid to a heap of gold we don't own. Gettin' it back is a problem for the law, not us.'

'OK,' said Sam with a shrug. 'I guess you both know better'n me.' He looked about and then said, 'They didn't leave any food either. Still it don't matter now, I reckon I can soon catch a rabbit or somethin'.'

They were about to unhitch their horses when Sam suddenly held Cobb's arm and looked intently downstream.

'I reckon we got company,' he said. 'Did you see them birds suddenly fly up in the air? Must've been twenty or thirty of 'em.'

'So what?' asked Williams.

'So what is that them type of birds don't normally flock together,' said Sam. 'You might get quite a few together when the weather's like this, but they ain't birds what flock together. No, sir, somethin' spooked 'em.'

'They could have been set up by almost anything,' said Cobb.

'No, Major,' insisted Sam. 'The only thing in these parts what'd spook them birds is somethin' like a man. They're used to everythin' else an' wouldn't take no notice. I reckon we got company right enough.'

'OK, Sam,' agreed Cobb. 'So far you've proved that you know more about what goes on out here than either of us. I'll take your word for it. All the more reason we should be on our way.'

'Sam has a point,' said Tom Williams. 'It might just be them four comin' back. If they see we've taken the horses they might just come after us. I say we hide up an' see what happens.'

'There's just one question I'd like to ask,' said Cobb. 'Why would they come back this way?'

'On account of they can't cross the creek,' said Sam. 'About four miles down it drops into a deep gully, maybe seventy feet deep. It's also joined by another creek half way along the gully. That creek will also be filled with water. There's no way they can cross. Only way is about two miles upstream from here an' only then if they're lucky.'

'So they could be forced back this way?' said Cobb. 'OK, get your hides up among those rocks and wait to see what happens. We leave everything else here.'

'All exceptin' my gun,' grinned Sam.

They had only just reached the safety of the rocks when four riders appeared and all were quickly identified as the four outlaws. They seemed to be riding past the wagon and the horses when one of them suddenly called a halt and pointed down at the ground. All four looked in their direction and drew their guns.

'So you didn't go to Geraldine,' called Jack Crane. 'Come on out, Major, we know it's you. The ground's too wet to hide your footprints.'

Cobb indicated that they should all keep quiet.

'Silence is it?' called Ed Bishop. 'OK, have it your way. We know exactly where you are and we've got guns an' you ain't, remember.'

'That's right,' called Jack Crane 'We gave you your chance; just can't say as we didn't. You should've headed for Geraldine while you could, at least that way you'd stay alive. This way you don't leave us no option.'

'Sam,' whispered Cobb, 'can you use that gun?'

'I'm as good a shot as most men,'

Sam whispered in reply. 'Only thing is this gun ain't been fired in maybe ten years; I only hope it works.'

'It's one hell of a time to tell us that,' grunted Williams. 'Still, I suppose we've got nothin' to lose.'

'Stand up real slow,' whispered Cobb. 'Sam, you hold back just behind us and make sure they can't see that gun. We'll walk down towards them and when I make a move, you get shooting. Let's just hope the darned thing does work.'

'I guess I'm as ready as I'll ever be,' said Sam.

The three of them stood up very slowly and moved away from the rocks.

'Have you ever killed a man in cold blood before?' called Cobb. 'That'd make it murder. I'm sure you don't want to be hunted with a price on your head, dead or alive. You said yourself that you weren't wanted for murder and wouldn't want to be. Think about it, Crane.'

'I've thought about it,' called Jack Crane. 'We reckon there's at least thirty thousand dollars in gold here. That kind of money makes a man's life seem very cheap.'

'I ask again,' called Cobb as they drew even closer, 'can you kill a man in cold blood?'

'If he can't, I can,' said one of the others. 'I've done it a couple of times. It's easy, all you do is point the gun like this . . . ' He raised his pistol and pointed it at Cobb. 'Then you squeeze the trigger like . . . '

The crack of a pistol being fired reverberated in Cobb's ear and the man pointing his gun at him suddenly dropped from his horse. In an instant, Cobb and Williams had thrown themselves behind a large rock and the remaining three outlaws were firing at them. The sudden gunfire had frightened their horses and it was plain that drawing a good line on Cobb, Williams and Coltrane was very difficult.

Cobb and Williams might have thrown themselves behind the only available rock but Sam Coltrane seemed oblivious to the danger and, laughing loudly, advanced on the riders. His gun fired at least twice and one more man, this time Ed Bishop, crashed to the ground. Suddenly Sam raced forward, snatched the gun now lying on the ground where the first man had fallen and threw it towards Cobb and Williams. Williams grabbed it, immediately broke his cover and succeeded in shooting the fourth man. By that time Cobb had also broken cover and snatched at Bishop's gun, and stood squarely facing Jack Crane.

'Hold it right where you are!' ordered Cobb. 'Unless you want to end up like your friends, you'll drop your gun. It's three against one now, Crane.'

'So I see,' said Crane, with a wry laugh. 'You asked me if I could kill a man in cold blood, Major, can you?'

'Just try me,' invited Cobb.

For a few moments Crane looked as though he might try to fight his way out, but suddenly he laughed and then threw down his gun and dismounted.

'I ain't no kind of hero, Major,' he said to Cobb. 'OK, this time you got the drop on me. I don't know where you got that other gun from but it just goes to show we didn't look hard enough. It's a pity really, I ain't never been that close to so much gold before in my life. As to whether or not I could have killed you in cold blood? No, Major, I don't think so, neither could Ed. The other two was different though. I know they've both killed unarmed men an' even a woman before.'

'Well that one won't be killing any more women,' said Cobb, pointing at the body nearest to him. 'It looks like he took it straight through his head.'

'This one's dead as well,' announced Tom Williams. 'Clean through the heart. That was a bit of fancy shootin' by Sam.'

'How about Ed Bishop?' asked Cobb.

'He looks like he'll live,' replied Williams, after he had checked him over. 'He'll have a sore shoulder for a while, but that's all.'

'Well done, Sam,' called Cobb. 'I don't know what we would have done if that gun of yours hadn't worked.'

'We'd all be lyin' there dead,' said Sam with a broad grin. 'What do we do with them now, Major?'

'We take them all back to Geraldine,' said Cobb. 'Tie Crane up, Tom,' he said to Williams. 'Sam, you get the others on to the wagon. I'll check their saddle-bags for the gold.'

Cobb soon had all the bags of gold back in the four boxes. Locking the boxes was, however, impossible since the locks had been shot off. Eventually, with Sam Coltrane driving the wagon containing the gold, two dead bodies, the injured Ed Bishop, Jack Crane and now with five horses in tow, they set off back in the direction they had come. Fortunately for them, by that time the ground had dried out and presented no problems for the wagon.

★ ★ ★

It took them just over two days to reach Geraldine, and Cobb was not at all surprised to discover that they were on the verge of sending out a search party. He explained what had happened to both the local sheriff and to a man who was obviously an official of the state. He also expressed his opinion that the whole thing had been set up by Captain John Fisher and possibly even Sheriff McGovan. The local sheriff seemed to pour scorn on the idea but the state official appeared to agree, although his main concern was for the gold.

Simon Jopson, a little, thin man, who peered at everyone through thick glass spectacles, fussed around and insisted that the gold must be lodged with the bank as soon as possible. However, bank opening hours being what they were and a relic from British colonial days, meant that it was closed. It apparently took some considerable cajoling and pleading to persuade the president to open his bank, but he eventually agreed.

While they waited for the bank president to make an appearance, Simon Jopson idly opened one of the bags of gold. Suddenly he cried out and poured the contents on to the table in the sheriff's office. He immediately opened another bag, felt at the contents and allowed them also to be poured on to the table.

'Sand!' he exclaimed. 'Sand, nothing but sand! What is the meaning of this, Major Cobb?'

'Sand!' repeated Cobb, grabbing at the sand now on the table.

'Yes, Major,' grated the little man. 'Sand! I demand an explanation.'

'Well, all I can say is we were sent to escort nothing more than a load of sand,' he said. 'Is it all sand?'

Between them, they soon had all the other bags emptied and they all contained nothing but fine sand.

'Well, Major!' repeated Jopson, 'I'm waiting for an explanation.'

'I don't know a thing about it,' insisted Cobb. 'You'd better ask Crane and Bishop. Maybe they made the switch.'

'That don't make sense,' said the sheriff. 'You had the best chance to switch it, I reckon you need to answer some questions.'

'And when might I have made the switch?' demanded Cobb. 'There were always four others around, including Crane and Bishop. I'm sorry, Sheriff, but I believe that there was never any gold in those boxes right from the start. We were all duped.'

'Are you suggesting that Captain Fisher deliberately substituted sand for the gold?' demanded Jopson. 'I find such a notion very hard to believe.'

'Then believe the evidence of your own eyes, Mr Jopson,' said Cobb. 'I think that Crane and Bishop might be able to throw some light on what really happened. Let's talk to them; it should make an interesting story.'

'I'll do the talkin',' insisted the sheriff. 'You wait here. Me an' Mr Jopson will talk to them. I don't want you tryin' to put words in their mouths. Jim . . . ' he said to his deputy, 'if he so much as makes one move, you shoot him, do you hear? Come on through, Mr Jopson, we'll soon have this sorted out.'

The two men went through to the cells but made no attempt to close the door and Cobb could hear exactly what was being said.

'That gold you stole,' said the sheriff. 'When did you make the switch?'

'Switch?' asked Crane. 'What the hell are you talkin' about, Sheriff?'

'I ain't here to play games,' said the sheriff. 'You switched that gold with sand, didn't you?'

'Sand!' exclaimed Crane. 'You gotta be jokin', Sheriff. Why the hell would we do a stupid thing like that?'

'You tell me,' replied the sheriff. 'The fact is it's all sand.'

'The bastard!' exclaimed Crane. 'Ed, you hear that? The bastard switched the gold for sand.'

'Who switched it?' demanded the sheriff.

'Fisher, of course,' said Crane. 'Who the hell else? Captain John Fisher. He must've done it. There ain't no other explanation.'

'What about Major Cobb?' asked Jopson.

'Naw, don't be stupid,' said Crane. 'Too damned honest.'

'I see,' said the sheriff. 'So what you are saying is that there was never any gold in the first place. Now why should Captain John Fisher send out a load of sand?'

'Plainly because he expected some-one to try and steal it,' said Jopson. 'That must be the explanation. He's probably on his way here with the real gold right now.'

'I wouldn't count on it,' said Crane, with a derisory laugh. 'I'd say that by now your Captain Fisher is well clear with somethin' like at least thirty thousand in gold, maybe even more.'

'Explain yourself!' ordered Jopson.

'OK, I will,' agreed Crane. 'I guess I'm goin' to be sent to prison for tryin' to steal the gold anyhow so I might as well tell you what I know. Me, Ed Bishop an' the other two made a deal with Captain Fisher. I didn't know much about the other two but Fisher seemed to know 'em all right. They was sent on ahead to meet us, just like they did. Anyhow, the deal was that we was to steal the gold and meet up with Fisher in Kingsville. He was to make certain that nobody knew where we'd gone. He was supposed to make it look like Major Cobb and the other two had stolen it. Anyhow, that was his side of the business an' not ours. We was to meet up in Kingsville an' divide the gold between the six of us.'

'Six of you?' queried Jopson.

'That's right, six of us,' said Crane. 'Oh, I forgot to tell you, Sheriff McGovan was in on the deal as well.'

'And you had no idea that what you actually stole was nothing but sand?' asked Jopson.

'None at all,' said Crane. 'Ain't that right, Ed?'

'That's it,' said Bishop. 'The bastard! He sold us down the river good an' proper.' He gave a loud groan. 'Sheriff, this shoulder is killin' me. Can you get a doctor to look at it?'

'All in good time,' said the sheriff. 'So Major Cobb, Tom Williams and Sam Coltrane had nothing to do with any of it?'

'Not a thing,' said Crane. 'One thing is for sure, none of them had the chance to switch the gold, me an' Ed kept an eye on them all the time.'

'Very well,' said Jopson, 'from what you say it would appear that Captain Fisher planned the whole thing.'

'I'm puzzled about one thing,' said the sheriff. 'Why didn't you kill the major, Williams and Coltrane while you had the chance? That way there would have been nobody to testify against you.'

Jack Crane laughed and shook his head. 'That's what was supposed to happen, Sheriff. Me an' Ed might've robbed a good many folk, shopkeepers an' homesteaders an' the like, but neither of us ain't never murdered nobody. Before we left I told the other two that murder was out of the question an' that I would kill them both if they tried. Anyhow, it seems they bought the idea 'cos they didn't try to kill any of 'em when we took the gold — or what we thought was the gold. I know they'd both killed folk before, but they wasn't actually wanted for murder.'

'It would appear that you were lucky, Major,' the sheriff called out. 'OK, I guess we now know what happened. You can go if you want.'

'There's just the little matter about payment, Mr Jopson,' said Cobb. 'We were promised payment for this trip.'

'Under the circumstances, Major,' replied Jopson, coming back into the office, 'it would seem that you were more than fortunate to get away with your lives. Don't you consider that payment enough?'

'Mr Jopson,' said Cobb, with a deep

sigh. 'I don't think you quite understand. I was promised sixty dollars
— twenty dollars a day for three days.
Tom Williams and Sam Coltrane were
promised ten dollars a day. Now the
one thing we didn't know was that
there was no gold. Had we known that
it was only sand, do you think we would
have risked our lives trying to recover
it? No, Mr Jopson, I think you are
duty bound to honour your part of
the agreement. We certainly honoured
ours.'

Cobb had expected Simon Jopson to
protest and even refuse to pay them,
but suddenly he smiled and nodded.
He took a wad of notes from his pocket
and counted out $120.

'Never let it be said that I, Simon
Jopson, ever reneged on a deal,' he said.
'Very well, Major, I take your point.
Here is your money.'

'Thank you, Mr Jopson,' said Cobb,
plainly surprised. 'May I say that it's a
real pleasure doing business with an
honourable man.'

By that time, the president of the bank had arrived and, when told what had happened, was obviously very annoyed. He blamed both the sheriff and Simon Jopson for not checking on the gold before they sent for him. Cobb simply laughed as the three of them started to argue and he went outside where Tom Williams and Sam Coltrane were waiting.

'I got you your money,' said Cobb, handing each of them their cash. 'Jopson wasn't going to pay us but I convinced him that he was duty bound to honour the agreement.'

'Now that just goes to show the value of proper schoolin',' said Coltrane. 'If that'd been me I'd more'n likely blown my top an' maybe even threatened him with a gun. It makes me wish I'd done me some real book learnin'.'

'But you make up for it by knowing what to do out in the wilderness,' said Cobb. 'We can't all know everything. You can still learn to read and write though. It's never too late.'

'You know,' said Sam, 'I might even just do that. There's a widder woman back home what used to be a schoolteacher. I think she's taken quite a shine to me. Can't think why the hell she should though.'

'Women are strange creatures,' said Tom Williams. 'Believe me, I know: I've had me two wives.'

'What happened to the first one?' asked Cobb.

'Don't rightly know,' said Williams. 'I walked out on her more'n twenty years ago. I did the same on the second about five years ago. I guess I'm just not the marryin' type.'

Cobb smiled and decided that the finer points of law concerning marriage were not worth bothering with. He knew that it was quite common for husband and wife to split up without divorcing and then go on to marry again.

'OK, Major,' said Coltrane, 'at least we got our money, our horses an' our guns. I guess you'll be on your way. It's been a pleasure knowin' you. I'll even let you buy me a drink.'

Both Cobb and Tom Williams laughed, slapped Coltrane on the back and steered him in the direction of the saloon.

'I suppose old habits die hard,' said Cobb, as they sat at a table with their drinks. 'You can't help bummin' a drink off anyone, can you?'

'I'm more than surprised that you were able to go without a drink for so long,' said Williams. 'It just goes to show you don't have to drink if you don't want to.'

'Sure, I know that,' said Coltrane. 'It's just that I don't want to.'

5

After a good night in one of Geraldine's two hotels, Cobb was wondering what to do and where to go next. He did not have any plans despite his years in the army when organization counted for everything. Planning ahead did not come as second nature to him and the style of his life since leaving the army meant that there was really nothing of any importance for which to plan. He wandered almost absentmindedly down the street when he was suddenly aware of someone calling his name. He looked around and saw the sheriff at the door to his office.

'I was kind of hoping you hadn't left town,' said the sheriff. 'Come on inside, I want to talk to you.'

Cobb nodded and followed the sheriff into his office where he was quite surprised to discover Simon Jopson.

'Morning, Mr Jopson,' acknowledged Cobb. 'Seeing you here tells me that this is something official.'

'I suppose you could say that, Major,' replied Jopson. 'Please sit down.' Cobb did as asked and Jopson leaned forward, placed his hands flat together and then put his fingertips to his lips as if in prayer and gazed at Cobb for a few moments. 'We have a problem, Major,' he suddenly said. 'I have tried to contact Captain Fisher but have not been able to do so,'

'That's hardly surprising is it?' said Cobb. 'I'd say he was well away with a whole lot of gold right now.'

'Yes,' muttered Jopson, 'It would appear so. It would also appear that he has taken about fifty thousand dollars in cash.'

'In cash!' exclaimed Cobb. 'All that gold and fifty thousand in cash? He certainly doesn't do things by halves, does he?'

'Precisely, Major,' said Jopson. 'That is the problem, or at least part of it.'

'And the other part?' asked Cobb.

'The other part is that at this precise moment we do not have anyone to send after him,' said Jopson.

'I thought you had the army at your disposal,' said Cobb. 'At least that was the impression I was given by Fisher.'

'Ordinarily I would be able to call upon a company of soldiers who are based near Geraldine,' said Jopson. 'However, as of yesterday they are deployed up in the mountains along with other soldiers from Fort Patterson, leaving only one man at Geraldine. I believe that Captain Fisher was also aware of this fact and indeed planned his movements accordingly.'

'Can't you get hold of them?' asked Cobb.

'I have been in contact with Fort Patterson and there are only five men remaining there, a corporal and four troopers. They are under strict orders not to leave. Apparently the main body of troops has been called out to deal with some renegade Indians who have been causing mayhem amongst settlers. Nobody knows of the exact location or movements of the renegades which means that the troops could be almost anywhere. All that was known by the corporal at the fort was that the soldiers were heading for the Rocky Mountains.'

'And that's a mighty big area,' said Cobb. 'I know, I've been up there a few times. A man can go for weeks and not see another soul.'

'Precisely, Major,' said Jopson.

'OK, so you've got a problem, Mr Jopson,' said Cobb with a sinking feeling in his heart. 'Just how does this involve me?'

'I need hardly tell you then,' said Jopson, 'that the Rocky Mountains and the soldiers from Fort Patterson are due west and that Captain Fisher is now undoubtedly due east. That puts a lot of time and distance between them both.'

'Surely there must be other army

posts?' said Cobb.

'Indeed there are,' agreed Jopson, 'and they have been warned to look out for the captain. That brings us to another problem: the governor of this state has a good understanding and agreement with the army and there is a great deal of co-operation but, unfortunately, that same arrangement does not extend beyond the border. Whilst the army will undoubtedly help if they can, they refuse to become deeply involved in what they claim is a civil matter. In other words they refuse to organize patrols especially to search for the captain.'

'That's standard military practice,' said Cobb. 'OK, so the army is out, what about the civil authority?'

'You mean a marshal,' said the sheriff. 'Unfortunately this state has not long been admitted to the union and at this moment we have only one US marshal assigned to us. Right now he is out chasing a gang who murdered almost everyone travelling in a small wagon train heading for California and we are unable to contact him.'

'Very convenient,' said Cobb. 'I still don't know what all this has to do with me though.' That was not true, he had a very good idea as to exactly what they were leading up to.

'Major,' said Jopson, 'in anticipation that you would not refuse, I am authorized to ask you to go after Captain Fisher and, if possible, apprehend him and recover the gold and cash he has apparently stolen. I am also authorized to promote you to the position of deputy US marshal. It is, of course, a purely temporary appointment, but you will receive the full pay of a deputy marshal for the duration of your appointment.'

'And if I refuse?' asked Cobb.

'Then that, most unfortunately for our part, is the end of the matter, Major,' said Jopson. 'The only thing I would add is that it would not be inconceivable, in view of your co-operation, that a favourable review of your dismissal from the army would take place.'

'You have been busy, Mr Jopson,' said Cobb. 'It didn't take you long to find out about my past. I'm quite certain that I never mentioned it to anyone. It's not something of which I am very proud.'

'I have my methods, and a certain amount of influence, Major,' said Jopson with a very straight face. 'As you are no doubt aware, a favourable review of the circumstances of your dismissal would, if upheld, mean that your pension rights and the right to use your rank would be fully restored. Technically, since you were cashiered, you are not allowed to refer to yourself as 'Major'.'

'I don't,' said Cobb. 'That's something everybody else seems to latch on to. OK, so I might and only might, agree, but there are certain conditions on my part as well.'

'I would have thought that what I have just offered would have gone a long way to meeting any objections you might have,' said Jopson. 'There is not much more that I can offer you.'

'How about ten per cent of the value of whatever I recover?' said Cobb. 'I believe ten per cent is the normal rate.'

'Assuming that you recover most of it, that could mean ten per cent of about one hundred thousand dollars,' mused Jopson. 'That is a lot of money, Major. I certainly do not have ten thousand dollars to look forward to despite my many years of service to the state.'

'But you're not expected to go out after a man who would kill you at first sight,' said Cobb. 'You will be quite safe behind your desk. Not only that but are you expecting me to go out there alone?'

'I am not authorized to appoint you any deputies,' said Jopson.

'OK, so *you're* not authorized,' said Cobb. 'I do know a little about how things work, Mr Jopson. If I take up the position, I can appoint my own providing I pay for them. That's another reason I need the ten per cent.'

'I am not certain that I can obtain permission for your request,' said Jopson. 'Is that your final word, *Mister* Cobb?'

Cobb did not miss the emphasis, but he felt that he had the upper hand.

'I'll put it this way, *Mister* Jopson,' he said. 'Your offer to have my case reviewed does not provide me with any guarantees. As far as the gold and the money are concerned it really is none of my business. OK, so you've lost a lot of money but that's your problem, not mine. I need rather more than the vague possibility of some review which might or might not end in my favour. Should it not happen, I certainly need more out of it than the pay of a deputy marshal for however long it takes. It's my life on the line, Mr Jopson, not yours.'

'Point taken, Major,' said Jopson. 'I shall contact my superiors and let you know what their reply is. I should have a reply by midday and I shall let you know whatever the outcome.'

Cobb left the office feeling that if nothing else he had scored some sort of moral victory over officialdom. Almost the first people he met after leaving the sheriff's office were Tom Williams and Sam Coltrane. Neither seemed surprised to see him.

'We seen the sheriff call you in,' said Sam, 'so we waited. From the look on your face I'd say he wasn't just passin' the time of day.'

'Let's talk,' said Cobb. 'It's too early for drinking even for you, Sam, so let's go and sit under that tree for a while.'

'Talk about what?' asked Tom Williams.

'Talk about hunting down Captain John Fisher,' said Cobb.

They sat beneath the tree where Cobb explained what had happened and, if he did agree, that he wanted both of them to go along with him. Sam Coltrane appeared to like the idea but Tom Williams was rather more cautious.

'It's OK for you, Major,' said Tom. 'Whatever happens you do get somethin' out of it. What do we get out of it? We might never find Fisher, or if we do he might have hidden the gold and the money and we'll never find it. We might even end up gettin' ourselves killed.'

'Getting yourself killed is one of the hazards of the kind of lifestyle you and I lead, Tom,' said Cobb. 'That's the deal. I quite understand if you want nothing to do with it and there will be no hard feelings on my part. I can't guarantee you a damned thing, I know that, but on the other hand what else have we got to do? I for one have precisely nothing to do and nowhere in particular to go, so I might as well be doing something which at least has the chance of something substantial at the end of it. In our own ways we're all looking for that elusive pot of gold at the end of the rainbow. If we don't find anything, at least we haven't lost anything.'

'I'm all for it, Major,' said Sam. 'Back home, I drank mainly 'cos I'd got nothin' else to do. It'd sure make a change from sittin' on my ass and drinkin' all day, an' I kinda like the idea of doin' somethin' useful for a change.'

'I'll have to think about it,' said Tom Williams. 'Ten per cent; maybe ten thousand dollars between us. What do we get out of it?'

'Three-way split,' said Cobb. 'Assuming we recover all the cash, that could mean anything between two and three thousand dollars each maybe even more. I'm quite sure that kind of money doesn't come your way too often. I know it certainly doesn't come my way all that often.'

'The thirty dollars we've just been paid don't come my way all that often either,' agreed Williams. 'I'll still have to think about it and let you know.'

'Whatever you decide, Major,' said Sam, 'you can count me in.'

At midday precisely Cobb was called into the sheriff's office again where he was told that ten per cent reward had been agreed in addition to which Cobb would be paid as deputy marshal for the period. The question of a review of his dismissal from the army was glossed over by Jopson claiming that it was a question which could only be answered by the military. Cobb was not too surprised at this and decided that the reward and the pay were probably the best he was going to get out of it and agreed to go after Captain John Fisher.

Much to his surprise, the badge of a deputy US marshal was produced and he was led across the street to the courtroom where he was sworn in by the local judge. He was also given a document confirming his temporary appointment. It appeared that Simon Jopson had prepared for just such an eventuality which made Cobb think that he, Jopson, had known of Fisher's possible involvement long before it had happened, but he decided not to question him further.

As he emerged from the courtroom, he was met by Tom Williams and Sam Coltrane. Coltrane looked at the marshal's star now pinned on Cobb's shirt with some envy.

'OK, Major,' said Williams, 'I've made my decision an' you've got yourself a deal. Like you say, I've got nothing better to do right now nor likely to have. When do we start?'

'Just as soon as we gather some supplies and I've had a chance to talk to Bishop and Crane. They might have some idea as to where Fisher could be heading. I'm going to try and get some money off Jopson as well, just to cover expenses.'

Much to his surprise, Jopson raised no objections to giving him twenty dollars with which to buy necessary equipment and food and he even agreed that it would not be counted as an advance against his pay.

At first, both Bishop and Crane were uncooperative but Cobb persisted.

'It seems to me that you are protecting the man responsible for you being where you are now,' said Cobb. 'I don't think I would be too kindly disposed towards any man who set me up with bags of sand instead of gold and then ran out on me leaving me to the prospect of a lengthy jail sentence. Remember, you haven't long been let out of prison and I don't suppose any judge will take too kindly to you re-offending quite so soon afterwards.'

'What's in it for us?' demanded Crane. 'Seems to me we get sent to prison no matter what happens.'

'Unfortunately there is nothing I can do about that,' said Cobb. 'That is something only the judge can decide. All I can say is that I will speak on your behalf and hope the judge takes your co-operation into account. I gather judges are usually quite reasonable with anyone who co-operates with the law.'

'Always assumin' you live to speak for us,' said Bishop. 'I can't see Fisher giving up without a fight.'

'I am quite certain that the sheriff and Mr Jopson will also testify that you have helped them,' said Cobb. 'I believe that Mr Jopson is a very influential man. He certainly appears to have access to some very confidential information and probably to people with great influence.'

'OK, Major,' said Crane with a deep sigh. 'I guess we got nothin' much to lose either way. We don't know that much really. Both me an' Ed was approached by Fisher not long after we both got out of prison. Oh, he didn't come right out with it. At first we was employed just like you was, as guards. It was only later he came up with the idea of stealin' the gold. Like fools, we agreed to go along with it. We was to get half of everything between us. He was goin' to take half as his share. We didn't mind that too much since he insisted that it meant at least twenty thousand dollars apiece. That's a lot of money to a man who ain't never had much, Major.'

'I gathered that it was probably something like that,' said Cobb. 'The important question is, did he ever mention any names, names of places, anything which might give me a lead?'

Both men thought for a few moments and then shook their heads.

'Naw,' said Bishop. 'I don't remember nothin'.'

'Me neither,' said Crane, 'except maybe just somethin' I overheard him sayin' to Sheriff McGovan. I seem to remember the name Paynes Creek or somethin' like that bein' talked about. I don't know where this Paynes Creek is, or even if that was where they was headed. All I know is I overheard the name, that's all.'

'Paynes Creek?' said Cobb. 'Are you quite sure that was it and are you certain that you have no idea where it might be?'

'No, sir,' said Crane. 'I ain't never heard of it.'

'OK,' said Cobb. 'Are you sure there's nothing else, anything at all, no matter how unimportant it seems to be?' Both men shook their heads. 'Where did he tell you to meet him?' continued Cobb.

'Turkey Bend,' said Bishop. 'We was to make our way to Turkey Bend an' wait for him.'

'Which probably meant that he never intended going there,' said Cobb. 'Very well, gentlemen, I thank you for what you have told me. It might be nothing, but at least it's something to go on. Should I not be able to get to court to speak on your behalf, I am quite certain that the sheriff here will testify as to what you have told me. I wish you the best of luck.'

'I reckon we're goin' to need all the luck we can get,' said Crane. 'There is just one more thing, Major. Now I think about it I seem to remember a woman's name bein' mentioned just the once when I walked in on them unexpected. That was just before we all left with what we thought was the gold. The name was Florence Wheeler. I'm certain that was the name. Yep, it was definitely Florence Wheeler. Don't ask who she is though, I ain't got the faintest idea. I never heard where or how she was involved. They saw me an' clammed up an' I didn't really think about it after that.'

The names Paynes Creek and Florence Wheeler meant nothing to the sheriff nor Simon Jopson. Sam Coltrane, on the other hand, was quite certain that he had heard the name Paynes Creek somewhere before although he could not remember where or when for the moment. He said that he would think hard about it. It also transpired that Sheriff McGovan had now disappeared, but Cobb was not surprised, in fact he would have been more surprised had he remained.

'I suggest that we go back and talk to McGovan's wife,' said Cobb. 'We don't have any other leads. She might be able to throw some light on this Paynes Creek and Florence Wheeler but I doubt it.'

* * *

Two days later, Cobb was talking to Sheriff McGovan's wife. No, she had never heard of either names and no, she had had no idea that Captain Fisher and her husband were planning to steal the gold and the money.

'I hope you don't mind me saying so, Mrs McGovan,' said Cobb, 'but you don't appear to be very upset by your husband's disappearance.'

'And of course, you are thinking that I am going to join him sometime,' she said, laughing wryly. 'Frankly, Mr Cobb,' she continued, 'I'm not at all sorry to see the back of him. He was a very jealous and very violent man. He would beat me if I so much as looked at another man, or even if he didn't like my cooking. The only man he didn't appear to be jealous of was Captain Fisher.' Again she laughed wryly. 'No, he wasn't jealous of the captain and believe me he probably had more cause to be worried about him and me than anyone else. No, before you jump to conclusions, the captain and I were not lovers, but he certainly tried his best and very nearly succeeded.'

'So you have no plans to join your husband?' said Cobb. 'His disappearance must mean that you have no money coming in now. How will you manage?'

'I have my own money, left to me by my father,' she said. 'It's not a fortune, but it is enough for me to live on in reasonable comfort. I always took care not to allow my husband anywhere near my inheritance simply because I felt that I would leave him one day. Besides, I am not an old woman and there are quite a few eligible men around.'

'I'm quite sure you will find yourself a good man,' agreed Cobb. 'Have you any idea in which direction either Captain Fisher or your husband went? I gather they did not leave at the same time.'

'I didn't see which way the captain went,' she said, 'but a neighbour, Martha Peters, saw my husband riding east on the day he disappeared. That's all I can tell you, Major. Please, do me a favour: if you do happen to catch my husband, *don't* bring him back here. It will make life so much easier and give me grounds for a divorce if he does not come back.'

'I can't promise anything,' said Cobb. 'Thanks for your help.'

'East,' Cobb said to his companions. 'That's the way McGovan went.'

'Fisher too,' said Tom Williams. 'I asked about and the general opinion is that he went east as well.'

'An' I ain't been idle,' said Sam. 'I been talkin' to an old fur trapper, name of Aaron Wingfoot. He's a half-breed, and I guess he can't help that, but they reckon he was one of the best fur trappers around in his day. I thought that if anybody should know where this Paynes Creek is he would, even though I was sure I'd heard of it. Anyhow, I remember now. He reckons there's a place called Paynes Creek about two hundred miles east which ties in with what I remember. He says it was nothin' but a stagin' post for the stagecoach company, when they used to run stages between Geraldine an' Harper City that was. They stopped them stages a few years ago on account of nobody was usin' it. He couldn't remember exactly where it was but I got me a pretty good idea how to get there.'

'Very well,' said Cobb, 'lead on Sam, we might as well start there as anywhere and hope that Fisher hasn't headed off in some other direction.'

★　★　★

Four days later, they came upon a battered sign leading off what was now the main trail which indicated that Paynes Creek was four miles along a narrow valley.

Paynes Creek itself had plainly seen better days, in fact it now comprised of five rickety buildings none of which were occupied and had plainly been empty for some considerable length of time.

The largest had a series of paddocks behind it, now with broken fences which seemed to confirm what the old trapper had said about it being a staging post. There was no sign of recent human habitation at all but there was other evidence of man's hand in the form of at least a dozen pigs which had now gone wild. Sam Coltrane lost no time in killing one of the smaller pigs and preparing it to be roasted. It was as he was gutting the pig alongside a small stream, presumably the creek from which Paynes Creek got its name, that he made his grim discovery.

'Major, Tom,' he called. 'Maybe you'd best come an' look for yourselves. If this is what I think it is, I reckon we've found Sheriff McGovan.'

The two men gazed down on what appeared to be fairly recent human remains under a bush. Quite plainly the body had been buried in a shallow grave under the bush in an attempt to hide it. Since then it had been unearthed, apparently by the pigs, and partially devoured by them. It was something Cobb had seen once before amongst some hill dwellers who apparently fed the remains of strangers they did not like to their pigs.

'You knew him better than we did,' Tom said to Sam. 'Is it him?'

'Folk look kind of different when they is dead,' said Sam, 'but sure, I'd say it was McGovan.' He pulled at the jacket and produced a sheriff's star. 'I guess that confirms it,' he said. 'There ain't too many folk what ride around with badges like these.'

'It's impossible to tell how he died,' said Cobb. 'The pigs have seen to that. I'd say he was shot though.'

'You know, I was quite lookin' forward to some decent pig meat,' said Tom, 'but all of a sudden I don't feel so hungry no more.'

'Don't see why not,' said Sam. 'I heard that human meat tastes exactly the same as pig meat anyhow. 'Sides, it's the pigs what have eaten him so you won't tell no difference. Hell, they eat some pretty strange things anyhow an' nobody don't bother about that.'

'That's not quite the point,' said Cobb. 'It looks like you'll be eating that pig on your own, Sam.'

'It don't bother me,' said Sam. 'I reckon you'll change your mind once you smell it cookin'.'

'Search the body,' said Cobb. 'See if there is anything which might indicate where they were planning to go.'

'Don't reckon there will be,' said Williams. 'It looks to me like killin' McGovan was what Fisher planned all along.'

'Well, look anyway,' said Cobb. 'At least we know one thing for certain, we are on the right trail. Let's hope that we catch up with him soon.'

As expected, there was nothing on the body to indicate where Fisher might have gone. Cobb now had to decide whether to go back to the main trail or to continue through the valley. According to Sam Coltrane, the route through the valley eventually led to a place called Harper City.

'I reckon he would've gone on to Harper City,' said Sam Coltrane. 'I know that's what I would do if I was him. He'll know by now that the army an' the law have been warned about him an' he'll want to avoid them if he can. The main trail is too well used an' I know there are at least three army posts that way. As far as I know there ain't nothin' like that out at Harper City. I went there once, when I was a kid, an' it warn't that big even though it called itself a city. One main street with a few houses an' a couple of stores, that's all.'

'That was a long time ago, Sam,' said Cobb. 'Things have a habit of changing.'

'Just like this place, Paynes Creek,' said Sam. 'I remembered where I'd heard the name. Talk was that Paynes Creek was goin' to become a big town.

Somethin' about the railroad comin' this way. Never did though.'

'No, that's plain enough to see,' said Tom Williams.

As predicted by Sam, both Cobb and Tom Williams changed their mind about eating the pig once it had been cooked.

ROSCOMMON COUNTY LIBRARY

6

The journey to Harper City took the best part of another two days and, as predicted by Sam, the name Harper City was something of a grandiose title for a town consisting of just one street.

However, despite its lack of size, it did support a sheriff, a bank, a gambling hall-cum-saloon, a livery stable, two stores, a barber's shop, which also provided hot baths, and what purported to be a hotel. They left their horses at the livery and Cobb booked rooms for the three of them at the hotel and was left with the impression that three residents at any one time was something of a rarity.

Sam and Tom went off to the saloon and Cobb to find the sheriff. After quite some time, he eventually discovered Sheriff Bart Wardle at a pool about half a mile from town where he was drowning worms on the end of a line which was tied to a fishing pole.

'Deputy Marshal Cobb,' said Cobb by way of introduction.

If he had expected the sheriff to be impressed he was greatly mistaken. The man simply looked up casually, nodded briefly and then spat a wad of something very unpleasant-looking on to the ground.

'That's what your badge says,' grunted the sheriff. 'What brings a deputy marshal into a godforsaken hole like Harper City?'

'A man named Captain John Fisher,' replied Cobb. 'I think he came this way not too long ago.'

'Yep,' slurped the sheriff, spitting out another evil-looking wad. 'Sure did, six days ago it was.'

For some strange reason Cobb was very surprised that the sheriff had so readily admitted to the fact. At first he put it down to respect for his new-found position. However, the sheriff's seemingly complete indifference made him think again.

'You remember him then?' said Cobb.

'Sure do,' drawled the sheriff. 'Just like I'll remember you. I won't remember you 'cos you is a deputy marshal, but 'cos there ain't that many strangers come through Harper City. Ain't no need unless you is lost. Harper City is on the main road to nowhere.'

'Haven't you had a message telling you that he was to be arrested?' asked Cobb. 'I understand all sheriffs and the military were warned that he was wanted for robbery.'

'Nope,' said the sheriff, apparently concentrating on the line in the water. 'But then that ain't surprisin', Harper City ain't got no telegraph.' He looked up at Cobb for a while. 'Robbery, you say? What he do, take some candy off some baby?'

'He's a cut above stealing candy,' said Cobb. 'He stole about one hundred thousand dollars in gold and cash.'

'One hundred thousand dollars,'

repeated the sheriff in an almost matter-of-fact tone, once again concentrating on the line in the water. 'That's one whole heap of money, Marshal. I never knew there was that much money in the world. You sure it was that much?'

'Quite certain,' said Cobb. 'Which way did he go when he left and, probably more importantly, did he say anything about where he was going?'

'East, an' nope,' said the sheriff, suddenly hauling on the fishing pole and then cursing. 'Missed him again!' he snarled. 'I'll get that critter one day.' He pulled in the line and examined the bare hook as though it was in some way to blame for his losing the fish. 'He's a big 'un,' he continued. 'Must be thirty pounds if he's one. Big catfish he is. I'll get him one day as sure as eggs is eggs.' He looked rather more closely at Cobb and grunted. 'Sorry I can't help, Marshal,' he said. 'He was only here one night an' I only spoke to him once. I didn't see him leave but the only way he could've gone is east, there ain't no other way unless he went back the way he came.'

'But he did say that his name was Fisher, Captain John Fisher?' asked Cobb.

'Not to me he didn't,' said the sheriff. 'That's what he told Liz Cooper in the saloon.'

'Liz Cooper?' queried Cobb.

'Yep,' grunted the sheriff. 'She's one of the three girls what Mick provides for entertainment. Sometimes they dance, sometimes one of 'em sings, but most times they lie flat on their backs while customers poke at 'em.'

'I wouldn't have thought Harper City was big enough to provide such services,' said Cobb. 'Mind you, I did see a new building being erected so something must be going on.'

'That'd be the new minin' supplies store,' said the sheriff. 'Time was when Harper City had big plans. Old Mr Harper — he founded the city — tried to get the railroad to come this way, an' for a time it looked like it was goin' to, then they changed their minds. In the last two years though there's been a big change. They discovered big deposits of iron ore up in the hills an' now the miners come into town every Friday night, Saturday an' Sunday to spend their hard-earned cash. Mind, they're a canny lot, foreigners from somewheres called China most of 'em are. Funny little yeller-skinned folk with slanted eyes, but I guess they can't help that. There's others from somewheres called Russia. That's in Europe — wherever that is. I hear tell it's right across what they call the Atlantic Ocean. That's a mighty big lake full of water what you can't drink on account of it's full of salt. Anyhow, it's one hell of a long way away. Most of 'em don't even speak English an' they sure don't like spendin' too much money so three girls is plenty. They do buy other things though, so I guess it ain't too bad. Main thing is they don't cause much trouble, 'specially the Chinese. Them Russians can be pretty damned mean if someone crosses 'em though.'

'All very interesting,' said Cobb. 'Right now, however, I'm only interested in where Captain John Fisher is going. I'll go and talk to this Liz Cooper; he might have said something to her.'

'He sure didn't mention his money,' said the sheriff. 'If'n he had done Liz would've been after him straight away.'

Cobb left Sheriff Bart Wardle to apply another worm to his hook and move to a different part of the pool in his quest for the elusive catfish.

He found Sam and Tom at the bar of the saloon where one of the girls was attempting to lure Tom upstairs. She appeared rather concerned when she saw the badge Cobb was wearing.

'Liz Cooper?' Cobb asked the girl.

'Who wants to know?' she asked.

'I do, Deputy US Marshal Cobb,' replied Cobb.

'Sure, I'm Liz Cooper,' she pouted. She glared at Tom. 'You never told me you were lawmen. I don't like lawmen, at least I don't like marshals . . . ' She glowered at Cobb. 'Or deputy marshals.'

'Me an' him ain't,' said Tom, pointing at Sam. 'We just work for Marshal Cobb.'

'Same thing,' Liz pouted again. 'How'd you know my name, Marshal?' she demanded. 'I ain't done nothin' wrong.'

'I never said that you had,' said Cobb. 'Your sheriff told me that you had cause to entertain a certain Captain John Fisher a few days ago.'

'Considerin' the amount of time old Bart spends out at that fishin'-hole it's wonder he ever sees anythin',' she said. 'All the same, he seems to know everythin' what happens in Harper City. Sometimes he even seems to know before it's happened.'

'Well did you hire out your services to a certain Captain John Fisher?' asked Cobb.

'I guess that's one way of puttin' it,'

she said. 'I kinda like it — hirin' out my services. Sure it has a bit of class to it.'

'Just answer the marshal's question,' said Tom.

'OK, OK,' pouted Liz. 'Sure, Captain John Fisher did pay for the *hire of my services*. What's it to you? A girl's got to make a livin', an' there ain't no law against doin' what I do as far as I know.'

'Nor as far as I know,' said Cobb. 'I am not the slightest bit interested in how you earn a living, but I need to know anything Fisher might have said to you.'

'Man of few words, he was,' said Liz. 'Not much real action either, but I guess he got what he wanted. Anyhow, he seemed satisfied.'

'Did he give any indication as to where he was going?' persisted Cobb.

'Your friend talks real fancy, don't he?' Liz said to Tom and Sam.

'He was a major in the army,' explained Sam, as though he was quite proud of the fact.

'Major!' giggled Liz. 'I had me a colonel once. Ain't that higher than a major? I reckon it must be, he told me he was due to make general.'

'Did Fisher give you any indication as to where he was going?' demanded Cobb, beginning to lose patience.

'OK, OK, *Major!*' she scolded. 'No, he never said a darned thing. All I know is he headed east but then there's nothin' unusual in that. There's only two ways out of this hell hole. One's east an' the other's west. Only thing I can say is that he didn't seem all that short of money. I wouldn't've minded findin' out more about him, but I reckon he got what he paid for an' that was that. Ain't that just the story of my life? Men don't hang around long enough for me to get to know 'em.'

'My heart bleeds for you,' sneered Cobb. 'So, he didn't say much. There is one more thing. I don't suppose he mentioned the name Florence Wheeler?'

'Florence Wheeler!' she said with a

dry laugh. 'Marshal, when a man goes with me he don't ever think of another woman.'

'I take that as a no,' said Cobb. 'Thank you, Liz, that will be all.'

'Speak for yourself, Marshal,' she said, turning to Tom Williams. 'How about you, honey? I'd say it's been a long time since you had a woman.'

'Sure is,' admitted Tom. 'OK, lady, you got yourself a customer.'

Liz poked her tongue out at Cobb, took Tom by the arm and steered him up the stairs.

'I heard what you was askin' Liz,' said the bartender, as he collected a few glasses. 'You sure you got the name of that woman right, Florence Wheeler?'

'As sure as I can be about a woman I've never met,' said Cobb.

'Well, maybe that *is* her name,' said the bartender, 'but then again maybe you got it all wrong.'

'I'm listening,' said Cobb.

'Well, there's a Lake Wheeler about four days away,' said the bartender.

'You head east from here then take the north road from a tradin' post called McBurney's. It's about two days from there.'

'And what about the Florence part?' asked Cobb.

'That's just it, that's why I think you might have it all wrong, Marshal,' said the bartender. 'There's a small town on the lake what's called Florence. I ain't never been there but my mother was born there. That's how I know.'

Cobb digested this new information for a moment and eventually nodded. It was quite possible that Jack Crane had misheard the conversation and assumed that they were talking about a woman. It appeared to be an easy mistake to make.

'Four days,' said Cobb. 'OK, I'll go along with what you say since it was only a name we had and I'll admit that we did assume it to be a woman. Did you talk to Fisher at all?'

'Not to say really speak to him,' said the bartender. 'The only thing he seemed interested in was if there were any other towns, how far away they were an' if there were any army posts.'

'And are there?' asked Cobb.

'Nearest town is Pine Hills about three days due east, an' Florence on Lake Wheeler,' said the bartender. 'He never reacted at all when I mentioned the name Florence. Nearest army post as far as I know is Fort Warren just beyond Pine Hills.'

'Fort Warren I know,' said Cobb. 'I once had the misfortune to be stationed there for a few days. This was a long time ago though. I don't suppose he said anything else which might be useful?'

'Not a thing,' replied the bartender. 'Sorry I haven't been much help.'

'On the contrary,' said Cobb with a broad smile, 'you have been a great help. We might have just continued riding looking for a woman instead of a lake and a town. OK, Sam, what are you drinking?'

'Beer,' said Sam. 'They got the best

beer I've had in a long time, brewed right here on the premises.

'Make that two,' said Cobb.

Sometime later they were joined by Tom who looked very pleased with himself. Cobb bought him a beer and they sat at a table.

'Did she say anything else?' Cobb asked.

'She said it's a pity you is a marshal,' said Tom, grinning. 'She's got this thing against marshals ever since one killed the only feller she's ever had what wanted to marry her. Only other thing she did say was that Fisher wouldn't even let a bag he was carryin' out of his sight. She never did find out what was in it but she reckoned it was quite heavy. She wanted to know if we were after him because of the bag or what was in it.'

'Did you enlighten her?' asked Cobb.

'Nope, said I didn't know either,' said Tom.

'Well there's been a development since you went upstairs,' said Cobb. He went on to explain about the town on Lake Wheeler.

'Could well be, I suppose,' said Tom. 'Are you goin' to try it, or just put it down to coincidence?'

'I don't believe in coincidences like that,' said Cobb. 'If I ignore it we might be chasing around for months. Sure, we have to go and take a look if nothing else. At the worst we lose a few days, at the best we find Fisher, the gold and the money.'

★　★　★

McBurney's Trading Post proved to be a rather ramshackle building which housed a variety of goods and a large quantity of evil-smelling animal hides and furs. It transpired that most of his trade was through Indian hunters.

McBurney himself looked as decrepit as his surroundings and smelled almost as evil. Despite the man's appearance, Cobb had the uneasy feeling that he was not quite so simple or as decrepit as he appeared. At first the man looked at them with a very wary eye, especially when he saw the badge Cobb was wearing.

'Maybe he was through here, maybe he wasn't,' drawled McBurney. 'I don't ask no questions; it don't pay. I minds my own business like most folk in these parts. That way I get to live a bit longer.'

'You can't get many folk passing through here,' said Cobb. 'Don't tell me you can't be certain because I won't believe you.'

'Believe what the hell you've a mind to,' grunted McBurney. 'I don't give a shit either way.'

'I see you've got large quantities of whiskey and gin,' said Cobb, strolling round the store. 'Is that how you pay for your hides from the Indians? You must know as well as I do that it is illegal to sell whiskey or gin to the Indians.'

'So prove it,' challenged McBurney. 'It ain't only the Indians I deal with.'

'I don't think it would prove too difficult to establish,' said Cobb. 'I think I could get you closed down without too much trouble. Now, answer my question. Did a man called Captain John Fisher pass through here a few days ago and which way did he go when he left?'

McBurney obviously thought about telling Cobb to do his damnedest, but then apparently had second thoughts.

'Didn't say what his name was,' muttered McBurney. 'I never asked an' he never said. OK, so there was a feller through here six days ago. He wasn't your average drifter, in fact he didn't look like a drifter at all. It could've been him, I suppose.'

'That's better,' said Cobb. 'Now tell me what he said and which way he went and don't try telling me a pack of lies or else I might just come back and close you down.'

McBurney was plainly very uneasy and would not look Cobb in the eye.

'OK, Marshal,' he eventually said.

'He told me that it was quite possible that somebody would be lookin' for him but that I was to say he'd never been this way. He didn't say why an' I didn't ask. Anyhow, he got to talkin' to a couple of Indians what was here at the time. I never heard what they was sayin' but I do know that he must've paid 'em for somethin' 'cos immediately after he'd gone they suddenly had enough money to buy a load of whiskey an' some other things.'

'And why would he do that?' asked Tom.

'Them Indians would do almost anythin' for money or whiskey,' said McBurney. 'I reckon he paid 'em to deal with anyone who might be followin' him.'

'Deal with them?' demanded Cobb. 'Do you mean kill them?'

'Most likely,' admitted McBurney. 'I know most of 'em wouldn't think twice about slittin' a man's throat for nothin' more'n a single glass of whiskey. Anyhow, he headed north towards Lake Wheeler.'

'That's what I thought,' said Cobb.

'There's just one thing I don't understand,' said Sam. 'OK, so he paid them Indians to kill us. How could he be sure they would? I mean, wouldn't it be a simple thing for them to take the money and forget all about it?'

'Don't ask me,' said McBurney. 'I'm just tellin' you what happened, that's all. I ain't no mind-reader. Anyhow, them two do most of their huntin' between here an' Lake Wheeler.'

'This town Florence,' said Cobb. 'How big is it?'

'Not big enough to have a sheriff,' said McBurney. 'Mind you, neither is Harper City but they got one, for all the use he is. I ain't been up to Florence in more'n a year but I don't reckon it's changed all that much. I'd say at least half the folk there are Indians or half-breeds.'

'OK, Mr McBurney,' said Cobb. 'Thank you for the information. Just remember what I said about selling whiskey to the Indians.'

'I heard you, Marshal,' grumbled McBurney. 'I don't get too many strangers passin' through but when they do, I usually sell 'em somethin' even if it's only a bottle of whiskey or gin. Sometimes they buy food off me. Are you hungry?'

'What you got?' asked Tom.

'I got me some stew,' said McBurney. 'Good an' hot. Got me a woman out back an' she's a damned good cook for a squaw.'

'Squaw?' queried Tom.

'Sure. Out here a man takes whatever woman he can find,' said McBurney.

'I wouldn't touch his stew if'n I was you,' warned Sam. 'I was in a tradin' post over at Yuma once an' he made his stew out of the scrapin's from the hides he traded in. I reckon he must've poisoned a good many folk without knowin' it.'

'My woman uses only the best meat,' objected McBurney.

'Nevertheless, I think we'll give it a miss,' said Cobb. 'Thank you, Mr McBurney, we'll be on our way.'

'You can even have my woman for a dollar a time,' offered McBurney.

'That's another luxury we can easily miss,' said Cobb. 'Remember, no more whiskey or gin to the Indians.'

'Is that right about sellin' whiskey to the Indians?' asked Sam, as they left.

'I think so,' said Cobb. 'I know it's the law in some other states so I guessed it was the law here as well. Anyhow, he seemed to know it was.'

'And can you close him down?' asked Tom.

'That was pure bluff,' admitted Cobb. 'I don't know how I would go about doing something like that and frankly I don't care.'

'Well, it seemed to work,' said Tom. 'Let's hope that he was telling the truth about Fisher heading for Florence.'

'I think he was telling the truth,' said Cobb, 'but I don't trust the man.'

'Are you expectin' trouble from him?' asked Sam.

'I'm not at all certain what to expect,' said Cobb. 'Just keep your ears open and your eyes peeled, that's all.'

They had travelled only about a mile and a half when Cobb's doubts were suddenly a reality.

They were crossing a stretch of open ground with very little in the way of cover when a shot echoed round and Tom fell from his horse. Immediately both Cobb and Sam leapt off their horses and flattened themselves on the ground.

'Tom are you OK?' called Cobb.

'I'll live,' replied Tom. 'I took a bullet in my arm, that's all. Can you draw a line on him?'

'No,' admitted Cobb. 'I think he's somewhere among those rocks, but I can't be certain. Have you any idea, Sam?'

'He's up there, all right,' said Sam. 'How the hell we get to him though is a different matter. He's got us well an'

148

truly pinned down.'

'It has to be McBurney,' said Cobb. 'Nobody else knows we're here.'

'Well, we can't just lie here,' said Cobb. 'Tom, you stay where you are; Sam, you try and circle round to the right. I'll make my way round to the left. Can you manage a rifle, Tom?'

'Well enough,' said Tom. 'OK, I'll cover you.'

'There's not much cover,' said Sam. 'We're probably about a hundred yards from where he is an' at that range it's goin' to take some pretty good shootin' to take us out. What do you think, Major? You're the expert.'

'I wasn't in the cavalry,' said Cobb, 'I was an engineer, but it makes sense to me. The fact that he didn't kill you, Tom, must mean that he's not such a good shot or we are at the limit of his range. I suppose we don't really have much choice in the matter. OK, Sam, when I give the word, we both run like hell for the rocks. Tom, we are both relying on you.'

'If he's there, I'll see him,' assured Tom. 'I was the best shot in my unit.'

'OK, let's go!' said Cobb. 'I don't think I need to tell you to zig-zag, Sam.'

Suddenly both men broke what little cover they had and were running towards the rocks taking a zig-zag course. There followed several shots and although Cobb had to assume that some were aimed at him, he was not hit and was not aware of any bullets nearby. He threw himself behind a large rock, waited for a moment until the shooting stopped and called out.

'That was a stupid thing to do, McBurney!' he called. 'You should have known you couldn't hope to take the three of us. Are you OK, Sam?'

'I took a nick in the arm,' said Sam, 'nothin' more. I thought he was dead, but I was wrong. Major, he ain't dead but he soon will be from what I can see.'

Cobb joined Sam to see McBurney gazing up at them. He had a large, bloody wound in the side of his head.

'So the Indians weren't told to kill

us,' said Cobb, 'it was you.'

'Them too,' croaked McBurney. 'I guess you just got lucky, Marshal. I don't normally miss.'

'Why?' said Cobb.

'For one thousand reasons,' croaked McBurney. 'Fisher offered a thousand dollars if we killed anyone following him . . . ' He coughed up some blood. 'He didn't know for certain but he said he was just playin' safe. He gave me an' the Indians a hundred dollars with the promise of a thousand more.'

'Was a thousand dollars worth dying for?' asked Cobb. 'How and when were you to collect the rest of it?'

'All we had to do was take your bodies to Florence,' spluttered McBurney. 'A thousand dollars! I ain't never seen that kind of money in my life.'

'And now you're dying you'll never see it anyway,' said Cobb.

'Guess it was kinda stupid,' moaned McBurney, sighing deeply. He coughed up some blood and his eyes closed.

McBurney was dead.

7

'What I want to know is how the hell did he get in front of us?' said Cobb. 'He was still at the trading post when we left.'

'Then there has to be a quicker way here,' said Sam. 'I'll go take a look around. You go take a look at Tom an' see how bad he is.'

Tom's wound did not look too serious and Cobb bound it tightly using Tom's neckerchief. Both men looked up to see Sam leading a horse.

'There's a narrow gully back there,' explained Sam. 'From what I can see it passes between them two hills. The way we came is almost a full circle from the tradin' post. I noticed that at the time but didn't think nothin' of it. He just cut across. What we goin' to do with his body?'

'We take it back to the trading post,'

152

said Cobb. 'He said there was a woman back there. What she does with the body is up to her.'

The woman, surprisingly young, either could not speak English or was refusing to speak at all. She simply glared at them as they led McBurney's horse, with his body across it, to her.

'Here's your man,' said Cobb. 'I don't know what you know about all this, but maybe you'd better warn anyone else who cares to try and kill us that we don't die so easily.' The woman said nothing but continued to glare at them. 'OK, we've done our civic duty,' continued Cobb. 'Let's get out of here. I don't think there's much point in questioning her, she either can't speak English, or she'll just act dumb. Be ready for more trouble. It might happen any time.'

The remainder of that day passed uneventfully and that night they made camp amongst a clump of thorn bushes beside a small stream. Sam announced that he had seen some deer and was going after one. Neither Cobb nor Tom had seen anything, but then again they had not been looking for deer.

Sam had been gone for about fifteen minutes when they heard a shot and immediately they both snatched at their rifles and took cover. Five minutes later Sam returned and dumped the carcass of a small deer in front of them.

'Easiest huntin' I ever done,' said Sam. 'They just looked at me an' made no attempt to run.'

'Let's hope nobody else heard the shot,' said Tom. 'I reckon they might've done though, I've had this feelin' that we're bein' watched for some time now an' I've long since learned my feelin's are usually right.'

'I didn't see nobody,' said Sam. 'I seen some old tracks but I reckon they are old, at least a week. An old Indian taught me to read signs when I was a kid. It's somethin' that never leaves you once you've learned.'

'I hope you're wrong about being watched,' said Cobb. 'But, just in case, I think one of us ought to keep watch all night.'

'I'll take last watch,' said Sam. 'I'm normally awake well before dawn anyhow. Does this mean we can't light a fire to cook anythin' an' I've been wastin' my time shootin' the deer?'

'I don't think we need go that far, Sam,' said Cobb. 'If there is anyone out there and they have seen us, it will look strange if we don't carry on as normal. They'll put two an' two together and know we know they're there. I don't want to alert anyone at this moment.'

'I don't think whoever it is will try anythin' here,' said Tom. 'Apart from these thorn bushes there's no cover for at least two hundred yards all around. Which watch do you want, Major?'

'We'll toss a coin for it,' said Cobb, taking a coin out of his pocket. 'Your call Tom.' Tom called heads as the coin was spun. It came down heads. 'I suppose that means I take the middle watch,' said Cobb.

★ ★ ★

Not too surprisingly, the night passed without incident and they were on their way as dawn broke the following morning, taking some of the deer meat with them for later consumption. The remains were left to a solitary buzzard which had taken up residence overlooking their camp and which swooped down on the carcass almost as soon as they had mounted their horses.

As they rode away, Cobb also had the feeling that they were being watched but look as he might, there was no sign of anyone. He eventually put his feelings down to the fact that Tom had mentioned it and nothing more.

They rode until about midday when they stopped on the top of a small hill which gave them a good view of the surrounding country which had now become largely dry brush. Tom was still insistent that they were being followed but there was no sign of anyone or anything. This did not really surprise

Cobb since he knew from experience that in such country it was even possible to be no more than ten yards away from someone on horseback and not be able to see them.

'I wonder how much further it is to this Florence place?' said Cobb. 'You seem to know most things about the wilderness, Sam, have you any idea?'

'I ain't never been this way in my life,' said Sam. 'This time, Major, your guess is as good as mine.'

'Two days from the tradin' post, that's what the bartender in Harper City said,' said Tom. 'I guess that means we should reach it sometime tomorrow.' He shielded his eyes and looked in the direction they were travelling. 'It looks like it turns into forest once we reach them mountains. They don't look far away.'

'Further than you might think,' said Sam. 'Out here distances never look as far as they really are. I reckon we'll be lucky if we reach them mountains by nightfall.'

'Then I think that if there is anyone following us,' said Cobb, 'they won't make their move until we're in the forest. If it is the Indians, they'll know this land like the back of their hands and they probably know that we've killed McBurney and won't risk anything in open country.'

'I'd say you were right, Major,' said Sam. 'In fact they've probably left us now an' gone on ahead. I suggest that even if we do reach the forest before nightfall, we stop short of it for the night, somewheres we can see what's goin' on an' where there's some cover just in case they do decide to try an' take us out.'

'Agreed,' said Cobb. 'OK, let's go. You are a man of some surprising abilities, Sam, what are your forest skills like?'

'I ain't got none,' admitted Sam. 'I never did like too many trees about so I never learned.'

'So it's a case of the blind leading the blind,' mused Cobb.

By the time the first signs of nightfall were evident, they still had not reached the forest, but it was now plainly visible about five miles ahead. Tom had to admit that his feeling of being followed had deserted him from about the time they had rested up at midday, which appeared to confirm Sam's suggestion that whoever it was had gone on ahead to lie in wait for them.

That night they made camp at the side of a small lake and ate the remainder of the deer. Once again they made no attempt to hide the fact that they were there and lit a fire, but they did agree to post a watch during the night. Once again Sam took the last watch while Cobb took the first. The night passed without any problems.

*   *   *

An hour after sunrise they came to the edge of the forest, following a fairly well-worn trail. Immediately they entered the forest all three had their handguns ready to use and their rifles resting across their legs. For almost an hour there was no sign of anything unusual.

The sudden crash of something in the undergrowth a short distance ahead of them had them all raising their rifles ready to shoot. Eventually Sam laughed and said that it must have been an animal of some kind.

'Don't ask me what it was,' said Sam. 'This is bear an' wolf country but I don't reckon it was a wolf, they don't make that much noise. More'n like it was a bear crashin' about. They don't care on account of not many things hunt 'em. Wolves might have a go at the cubs but they wouldn't dare tackle a full grown bear. They've got real mean claws what can rip a wolf apart in no time at all.'

'I don't trust bears,' muttered Tom. 'I had one charge me once for no reason at all. I was lucky I wasn't killed.'

'Funny animals is bears,' said Sam. 'Sometimes they'll just walk on by an' completely ignore you, an' other times they'll charge for no reason at all. Worst ones are mothers with cubs.'

'I agree,' said Cobb. 'It must have been something like that. I don't think any Indian would make that much noise. OK, keep going, but from now on keep your eyes skinned. If those damned Indians are about they could be anywhere. Sam, you seem best suited for this kind of thing, you take the lead.'

Sam did as instructed and for about another hour they travelled slowly, all the time looking and listening. At the end of that time Sam suddenly held up his hand and motioned them to remain silent. All three listened intently for some time before Sam eventually nodded and pointed to his right up a sharp, wooded slope.

'I think there's somethin' or somebody up there,' he whispered. 'You two take cover down here, I'm goin' up to take a look.'

All three dismounted and Tom and

Cobb took up position behind a fallen tree as Sam very slowly made his way in a circle round the slope. Cobb marvelled that for such a large and in many ways clumsy man, Sam moved very swiftly and very silently. In a short time Sam was lost from sight.

'Maybe we all should've gone,' whispered Tom. 'If he does meet trouble he might be outgunned.'

'I don't think we need worry too much about Sam,' said Cobb. 'In a town he's nothing but a clumsy oaf but out here he seems to be in his element. We'll give him another ten minutes. If he isn't back then we'll go and look for him.'

It was less than ten minutes later when they were both snatching at their rifles as they heard the sound of someone moving, this time behind them, in the opposite direction to that which Sam had taken.

'Hold your fire!' hissed a voice. 'It's me, Sam.'

'You stupid bastard!' said Tom. 'You

162

could easily have got yourself killed comin' in behind us like that.'

'Just checkin' around,' said Sam, apparently unconcerned. 'There was somebody up there an' not too long ago either. They'd had a fire an' it was still warm. I reckon they must've heard us an' moved on. I found horse tracks leadin' the way we're goin'. They can't be too far ahead of us.'

'Any idea who?' asked Cobb.

'Nope,' said Sam. 'My trackin' skills don't include bein' able to tell who they are. All I can say is that there are two of 'em. I'm quite sure of that. They'd killed a deer as well, but it looks like they didn't have time to pack up the remains.'

'Well now we know there's somebody there,' said Cobb, 'and we also know that they are aware of us and probably have been all along. I'd say they came on ahead knowing full well that this was the only way we could go.'

'I'll go along with that, Major,' said Tom. 'What do we do now?'

'Well, the one thing the army did teach me was never to present an easy target,' said Cobb. 'I suggest that we ride abreast, one of us along the track and one either side, say about ten yards between us. It doesn't look too difficult ahead and that way one of us might see something.'

'OK, Major,' said Sam. 'I'll take the higher ground, you take the track an' I suggest that Tom takes the lower ground. Chances are that if they are lyin' in wait, they'll position themselves above us where the trees are bit thinner. I know that's what I'd do.'

'I agree,' said Cobb. 'Just be ready for anything. Shoot if you suspect anything at all. Don't take any chances.'

They split up and rode very slowly forward for some time. Suddenly, Sam called out and there were several shots. Immediately both Cobb and Tom leapt off their horses and ran in the direction of the shooting. They discovered Sam crouching behind a fallen branch and took cover alongside him. He was apparently unhurt.

'Like the man said,' said Sam, 'two Indians. I came across 'em hidin' behind this branch. It looked to me like they was ready to take us out. I think I surprised 'em by comin' above 'em. Anyhow, they ran off. I don't think they had time to get to their horses.'

'No they didn't,' said Tom. 'I can see one horse over behind that bush.'

'I'm surprised,' said Cobb. 'They don't seem very adept. Most Indians I ever met have been good in situations like this.'

'They looked like a couple of old men to me,' said Sam. 'I'd say it was a long time ago since they acted like proper Indians. There's a lot of 'em out at Kingsville, but they've mostly forgotten the old ways. Livin' in towns an' plenty of whiskey has dulled their senses. They shouldn't be too much trouble.'

'They were good enough to follow us without us seein' them,' reminded Tom. 'They can't've forgotten everythin'.'

'They're probably used to trackin' animals,' said Sam, 'but in other ways they've gone soft. The thing is, I reckon it's them what's runnin' scared now, not us, which gives us the edge.'

'Are we goin' after 'em, Major?' asked Tom.

'No, leave them alone. We've probably scared them off,' said Cobb.

'You could be right,' said Tom, 'but if they've been offered a thousand dollars to kill us, I can't see 'em givin' up that easy.'

'Neither can I,' agreed Sam. 'I say we go after 'em while they is runnin' scared. We might not get a better chance.'

'And I say we wait and see what they do,' said Cobb. 'Come on, I don't want any arguing.'

'Yes, sir, Major Cobb, sir!' mocked Tom.

They retrieved their horses and continued along the trail, still taking a line abreast and about ten yards apart. For another hour they met with no resistance, but when a bullet thudded into a tree close to Sam's head, they once again leapt off their horses and took cover.

'I told you we should've gone after 'em before,' hissed Tom.

'And I think they've chosen just about the worst place to attack us,' said Cobb. 'Worst place for them, that is. Look up there, there's a cliff which must be thirty or forty feet high and I don't think they're at the top. That means they're cut off from one line of escape. Sam, circle round ahead, Tom you go up from the right and I'll go straight up. We should have them cornered.'

Neither man argued and Cobb gave them time to get into position before he made his way up the bank, using trees as cover. However, before he reached the cliff, two shots rang out from the direction Sam had taken.

'They won't be no more trouble,' called Sam. 'One of 'em is dead an' the other ain't far off.'

Cobb and Tom joined Sam at the same time and he pointed down into a small hollow beneath the cliff face. The Indians were certainly not young men, in fact they appeared to be very old. Cobb leant over the injured man who was bleeding profusely from a wound in his chest.

'Why were you trying to kill us?' he demanded.

The old man looked up and shook his head slightly. 'Thousand dollars!' he managed to say, hoarsely. 'Much money, thousand dollars.'

'Fisher, Captain John Fisher?' Cobb persisted.

The old man nodded weakly. 'Thousand dollars!' he croaked again. 'Much money.'

'Not enough,' said Cobb. 'Fisher, where is Fisher? Is he in Florence?'

The man nodded briefly. 'Thousand dollars!' he said again, as his eyes closed for the final time.

'What a waste of life,' muttered Cobb. 'Two old men, what a waste.'

'They was only Indians,' said Sam. 'Nobody don't care nothin' about no Indians. It wasn't that long ago there was a bounty on Indian scalps.'

'They were still men,' said Cobb, sadly. 'They couldn't help being what they are. You're right about them living in towns and going soft, Sam. I still think it was a pity they had to be killed.'

'I didn't have no choice,' said Sam. 'One of 'em was goin' to kill me.'

'Yes, Sam, I know,' said Cobb. 'They've probably got family somewhere. I think we ought to take them into Florence if nothing else.'

'Don't see why,' said Tom.

'But I do,' insisted Cobb. 'Get their horses and load up their bodies. It shouldn't take us too long to reach Florence now.'

Feeling that any immediate threat to their lives was past, they rode together along the trail with the two bodies slung across their horses. Two hours later Sam, who had ridden on ahead, motioned them to stop.

'Looks like we've reached this Florence place,' said Sam. 'Don't look much but it's probably a good place for somebody to hole up for a while.'

From a small hill, they looked down upon a group of houses and shacks situated alongside what appeared to be a large lake. There were several canoes tied up alongside a small jetty and several people were about their business in the town. From where they were it appeared that a large proportion of the inhabitants were Indians, although there were also a reasonable number of white faces.

'We stay here for a while,' said Cobb. 'I don't want to ride in there without warning. If Fisher is there I don't suppose he'll be too fussy about killing us. Keep an eye open, you might spot him.'

'That's always assumin' he's still there,' said Tom.

'That's a chance we'll just have to take,' said Cobb.

For more than two hours they all

studied the comings and goings of the citizens of Florence. During that time three canoes arrived and appeared to unload a catch of fish. Tom said that he thought he had seen somebody who looked very like Fisher, but he could not be certain.

'We can't stay up here all day,' said Sam. 'What plans have you, Major?'

'I've been thinking about that,' said Cobb. 'I think it's time we let Fisher know that we're here.'

'What the hell for?' demanded Tom. 'I say we just ride in an' flush him out.'

'Flushing him out is exactly what I had in mind,' said Cobb. 'There's a lot of people down there, far more than we could hope to deal with. We don't know whose side any of them are on.'

'OK,' said Tom, 'so what do you have in mind?'

'We've got two bodies,' said Cobb. 'I propose that we send them down into the town and watch what happens. Make sure that the bodies are tied securely, we don't want them falling off before they reach the town.'

'I'm with you, Major,' said Sam. 'Come on Tom, let's tie 'em up good.'

When Cobb was satisfied that the bodies would not fall off, the three of them led the horses further down the slope until they were within about 400 yards of the nearest building.

'OK, give the horses a good slap an' make them run into town,' said Cobb. 'Then we get back up where we can see what's going on.'

Tom and Sam gave the horses a good slapping and sent them off towards the town and, when Cobb was satisfied that they would not stop until they had reached the buildings, all three ran back up the slope.

They reached the clearing just in time to see the two horses racing along the solitary street, then being stopped by several of the residents. At first there was a lot of pointing in their direction and obviously a lot of shouting, although they were unable to hear what was being said. After a short time another figure appeared and after some more pointing in their direction Cobb was reasonably certain that it was Captain John Fisher. For a few minutes Fisher stood motionless, looking up in their direction. Eventually he disappeared. They could not be certain as to exactly where he had gone.

'That was Fisher all right,' said Cobb. 'Now let's wait and see what happens.'

The bodies were taken off the horses and taken into a nearby shed, but that apart, nothing else obvious did happen. Captain Fisher did not put in an appearance again, but Cobb had been prepared for something like this and had been keeping a look out just in case he tried to make good his escape.

There seemed to be only one way in and out of the town and that would bring anyone directly towards them. The only other means of escape appeared to be by canoe across the lake. Immediately behind the town and to their left, the slope was very steep, in parts almost sheer and even if somebody did try to go that way, there was a wide, treeless ridge they would be forced to negotiate. Cobb was quite confident that he would be able to see anyone going that way. To their right, the ground was very rocky, although there were plenty of trees but a cliff face about fifty feet high would force anyone using that route round to where they now were. He instructed Sam to reposition himself so that he could get a better view of that line of possible attack. However, it seemed that nobody was preparing to come up, most spending time in the street looking up in their direction.

'We seem to have them boxed in,' said Cobb. 'I haven't seen any sign of Fisher since though. I wonder where he is?'

'Headin' out across the lake,' said Tom, pointing down at the water. 'Look, there's a canoe just pulled out from under them trees.'

Sure enough, a single canoe had

moved away from the shore containing a lone figure. Cobb could not make out for definite who it was, but he was certain that it was not one of the Indians.

'That must be him!' he said. 'Sam, come on, we're heading for town.'

8

Their sudden arrival in the small town immediately created something of a panic amongst the residents even though they must have expected something since the bodies had been sent in. In fact, Cobb was at that moment wondering if they had done the right thing, but it was too late.

Most people ran to hide, fearing that they were being attacked for some reason. Most of the women either dragged or shouted at their children to follow them. There was one section of the population which did not appear frightened at all, two large and very vicious-looking dogs, although even they stood a respectful distance as they barked and snarled at the new arrivals.

At least six of the men had taken up defensive positions and seemed ready to shoot. Cobb raised his hand and called out, 'Hold your fire! I'm Deputy US Marshal Cobb, we don't mean you any harm.'

Very slowly and very cautiously the men emerged from their hiding places, but they still held their rifles at the ready. One of them eventually plucked up enough courage to walk over and examine Cobb's badge of office. He seemed satisfied and nodded to the others who then relaxed.

'You!' shouted Cobb, at one of the few residents who had not run away, an elderly white man, apparently completely unconcerned and who was sitting on the small jetty. 'That canoe out there, is that Fisher?'

'Could be,' admitted the man. 'Didn't see him leavin'.'

'You do know him then?' Cobb said.

'Sure, everybody knows him,' replied the man. 'Everybody knows everybody else in these parts. Deputy Marshal, you say? Was that you what sent them horses an' them bodies in?' He walked across and looked at Cobb's badge as if to confirm what the other man had seen and nodded his head. 'Everybody knew them as well,' he continued, 'but I guess it figures, Marshal, I allus said Fisher was up to no good an' them two would slit any man's throat for the price of a bottle of whiskey. They won't be missed.'

'We have to go after him,' Cobb said. 'I'm commandeering one of these canoes.'

'Take mine,' offered the man. 'That's it over there, the one with the eyes painted on the front.'

'Thanks, we will,' said Cobb. 'You can look after our horses. Where is he likely to be heading?'

'Straight across I reckon,' said the man. 'He's been across there a couple of times since he's been here. Don't know what the attraction is, there ain't nothin' on the other side 'ceptin' trees.'

'He might have a horse over there,' suggested Tom.

'Has he?' Cobb asked the man.

'Not that I know of,' he replied. 'Only

way a man could get a horse over there is by ridin' round an' that's more'n thirty miles of mighty slow goin'. I know that 'cos I did it once. I do know he ain't been that way since he's been here. Not this time anyhow.'

'Then we must assume that he hasn't got a horse over there,' said Cobb. 'What do you mean, *this time*?'

'Regular visitor over these past six months,' explained the man. 'Said he was a retired army officer; captain he said he was, an' that he was lookin' for somewheres he could come fishin' sometimes.'

'He *was* a captain,' confirmed Cobb. 'I wonder what the attraction across the lake was? There doesn't seem much point in going across if he didn't have to and especially if he doesn't have a horse over there.'

'Probably part of his plans to steal the gold,' said Tom. 'He does seem to have applied a large part of military logic to all this.'

'Probably,' agreed Cobb. 'If he has

been across a couple of times there must be a good reason for it; a man like Fisher wouldn't waste his time doing something just for the hell of it. Tom, Sam, have you ever paddled a canoe?'

'When I was a kid,' said Sam. 'Me an' my brother had a small one on the river. From what I remember it ain't all that difficult.'

'I was in one once, more'n ten years ago,' said Tom. 'That's all.'

'Then I guess we'll just have to manage,' said Cobb. 'I've never been in one in my life.'

He opened his saddle-bag and took out two boxes of bullets for his rifle and stuffed them down the front of his shirt. He told Tom and Sam to do the same. They did not need bullets for their handguns as they had enough in their gunbelts.

'OK, let's go,' he said to them. He called to the old man again. 'I don't suppose you have a sheriff round here?'

'Nope,' said the man. 'Nearest sheriff is out at Scottsboro, that's more'n a hundred miles. This is part of Scotts-boro County, but we don't see no sheriff very often. Last time was more'n four years ago when some outlaws was supposed to have headed this way. All there is over there is miles an' miles of trees, plenty of deer, bears, wolves an' squirrels, a few Indians an' a couple of homesteads used by trappers but we hardly ever see 'em, they allus go to Scottsboro.'

'The nearest town, is that Scotts-boro?' asked Cobb.

'Nearest town of any size,' said the man. 'There's a couple more small settlements along the lake about the same size as Florence that's all, but they is on this side. Most folk live this side of the lake on account of it's flatter this side an' a man can grow a few crops.' By that time Tom and Sam had unhitched the canoe, found an extra paddle and were waiting for Cobb.

'Make sure you look after these horses and saddles,' said Cobb. 'You'll get paid when we get back.'

'If you get back,' said the man.

'Then if we don't you've won yourself three horses and all the gear,' said Cobb. 'One saddle alone is probably worth more than your canoe.'

Cobb joined Tom and Sam and it was plain that none of them was used to canoes. They almost turned it over as they clambered into it but after a few moments they seemed to have mastered the art of keeping it upright and fairly steady. Their attempts to paddle away also showed their inexperience but with a little helpful advice from the old man, they were soon on their way.

By that time the canoe containing Captain John Fisher was well out into the lake and even though the three of them were paddling hard, Fisher appeared to be making better headway than they were. However, by the time they had travelled about 200 yards, they were starting to paddle with more rhythm and Cobb thought that they were beginning to make up some lost water.

Cobb was surprised at just how long the trip across the lake was taking. It did not appear to be all that far but the opposite bank still seemed as far away as ever. It took them almost half an hour before they reached what Cobb thought was the halfway point. In the meantime, Fisher appeared ominously close to his destination. Cobb urged the other two to paddle even harder.

They still had quite a distance to go when Fisher beached his canoe, stared at them for a few moments and then headed for the forest which commenced only a few yards away. Cobb once again urged his crew to paddle even harder.

★   ★   ★

They were within about 100 yards of the shore when the first bullet tore through the hide of the canoe, just missing Sam. This was quickly followed by several other shots at least four of which also ripped through the hide.

183

'He ain't tryn' to kill us,' called Tom, 'he's tryin' to sink us!'

'An' succeedin',' said Sam, as he tried in vain to plug a hole in the bottom of the canoe where a bullet had ripped through the side and the bottom but water was now pouring through in several places.

'Keep paddling!' ordered Cobb. 'We might just make it.'

Several more shots also tore more holes through both the side and bottom of the canoe and it was obvious that they were getting nowhere as the canoe slowly filled with water.

'What the hell do we do now?' called Tom. 'We don't stand a chance; he can pick us off whenever he chooses.'

'Just make sure you've got your rifles,' said Cobb. 'All we can do is swim.'

'There's just one problem with that, Major,' said Tom. 'I *can't* swim.'

'Well, this is one hell of a time to learn,' said Cobb. 'OK, I'll help you all I can. I take it you can swim, Sam?'

'Sure thing,' said Sam.

'OK, over the side,' ordered Cobb. 'Turn the canoe over if you can, that way it might float better with some air trapped in it and it will give us some cover. Tom, you hang on to it. When I say go, we all roll over this side' — he tapped the side furthest away from where Fisher was — 'pull it over if we can, an' then swim like hell for the shore using the canoe as cover.'

Turning the canoe over proved rather more difficult than Cobb had expected, but after three attempts, they finally had it upside down and apparently floating reasonably high in the water. Tom clung to the side whilst Sam and Cobb, rifles in one hand and gripping the side of the canoe with the other, thrashed their feet as they attempted to move towards the shore.

Several more shots ripped through the hide of the canoe, one of them dangerously close to Cobb's head, but they were beginning to make some headway if only very slowly.

Inevitably the canoe slowly started to sink as the trapped air escaped through the bullet holes, but by that time they were within about twenty yards of the shore. Finally the canoe disappeared completely. Cobb grabbed hold of Tom who, to his credit, did not panic as many non-swimmers might. It was then that Cobb realized that the shooting had stopped.

'OK, Tom,' he said. 'Hang on to me, only a few yards to go now.'

Sam, who was by then a couple of yards ahead of them, suddenly stood up. 'It's OK, Major,' he called. 'It's only about three feet deep.'

Tom breathed a sigh of relief as his feet also found the solid bottom and he released his hold on Cobb. 'Thanks, Major,' he choked. 'That was a close thing. I never did like water.'

'Fisher seems to have moved on,' said Cobb. 'At least he isn't shooting at us any more.'

'Don't rely on it,' warned Sam. 'Maybe he's just waitin' to get a better

186

line on us. I know that's what I'd be doin'. I had him among them rocks over there, but I reckon he could be anywhere by now. I only hope these rifles work after the soakin' they've had but don't rely on 'em.'

They scrambled on to the rocky shore and Cobb immediately ordered that they shelter behind a particularly large boulder to recover from their ordeal. Neither man argued with him and all three sank, exhausted, behind the boulder and between several other rocks for added protection.

'Well we can't stay here,' announced Cobb after a time and when they had recovered their breath. 'We've got a man to catch and some gold to find.'

'It's goin' to be dark before too long,' said Sam. 'Maybe we should wait for the mornin'.'

'Sam's right,' said Tom 'It seems like Fisher knows this area an' we don't. He could pick us off any time he wants to if we just go bargin' on.'

'He's close,' said Cobb. 'He's so close

I can almost taste him.'

'And I think he'll be just as close tomorrow mornin',' said Tom. 'You go on ahead if you've a mind to, Major, I reckon me an' Sam is just about jiggered; we need the rest. Anyhow, Sam was right about these guns seizin' up. I reckon we need to clean these rifles an' our pistols. There's no knowin' if they'll fire or not after bein' in the water. I know, I seen it happen before.'

'OK,' sighed Cobb, 'I suppose I'm out-voted. We rest up for the night. Before we do though, I want the canoe Fisher came in dragging up where we can keep an eye on it. I don't want him paddling back across the lake during the night.'

They hauled the canoe as far up the beach as they could and to where they could see it.

As the sun sank behind the mountains on the opposite side of the lake, it became distinctly chilly with a cold wind now blowing up the lake. They moved up the beach a few yards to the shelter of another large rock and a few trees, away from the wind. However, lighting a fire was completely out of the question according to both Cobb and Tom and not because they did not want to attract any attention. Whilst both of them had either matches or a tinder box, the soaking had done them no good whatsoever.

As ever though Sam had other ideas, and before long, after spending some time rubbing a long stick between his hands and on to a pile of dry grass, he soon had a fire going. Both Tom and Cobb admitted that they had tried to light a fire that way in the past but had never succeeded.

At last they now had shelter and warmth, but all three were feeling the pangs of hunger and, without thinking, both Cobb and Tom looked to Sam for an answer.

'OK,' said Sam with a wry laugh. 'I'll go see what I can find. I ain't promisin' nothin' this time though.'

'Just keep an ear open for Fisher,' warned Cobb. 'He could be anywhere and nothing would suit him better than to be able to pick us off one at a time.'

'You just worry about keepin' that fire goin',' said Sam. 'It's goin' to be a cold night, I can feel it already.'

Sam had been away for about ten minutes when a single shot rang out from somewhere amongst the trees and both Cobb and Tom grabbed at their rifles and crouched behind some rocks. There was only the one shot and eventually they heard someone coming towards them. Sam came into view carrying what appeared to be a small dog.

'Best I could do,' he announced as he dumped the carcass in front of them. 'Fox! Have either of you ever eaten fox?' Both shook their heads. 'Me neither,' admitted Sam. 'I suppose there's always a first time for everythin' though. Leastwise that's what my ma was always tellin' me. It's a good job I hit him with my first bullet as well.

Damned rifle jammed up on me after that. I had to finish him off with a knife. Damned thing bit me too.' He held up his hand for them to see a trickle of blood.

'Hardly what I'd call a bite,' said Cobb. 'OK, Sam, I'll try anything once. I mean, I have eaten pig that had been feeding on human meat.'

'I hear the Indians eat 'em, foxes that is,' said Sam. 'So if it's good enough for them it's good enough for me.'

'I wouldn't necessarily agree with that,' said Cobb. 'I once came across some Indians who lived way out in the desert and they used to eat anything that moved, including spiders and bugs. They had to, there was almost nothing else for them to eat. I never did try any bugs or spiders.'

'I reckon if you was hungry enough you'd eat 'em,' said Sam with a dry laugh. 'I know I would. In fact, me an' my brother ate some worms when we was kids. Not 'cos we was hungry mind, but 'cos we dared each other. We was like that, allus darin' each other to do stupid things. I can't say as they tasted all that bad. Secret is to swallow things like that, not to chew on 'em.'

'It seems to me you an' your brother tried most things,' said Tom. 'How about women?'

'Nope, never got round to that,' admitted Sam. 'Probably 'cos there warn't no girls around at the time. Anyhow, we wasn't all that interested in girls. I guess we was too young. We was more keen on explorin' an' things, just like most kids.'

The fox was skinned and roasted and, although the meat tasted quite strong, it was not too bad and it did satisfy their immediate hunger.

For safety, they once again agreed to take turns at keeping watch during the night and this time Cobb and Tom insisted that Sam take the middle watch. The fire was kept alight all night, which was perhaps as well since the night proved to be very cold.

The following morning, Sam claimed

that Fisher could not be too far away since he maintained he had detected the glow of a fire in the distance. Both Cobb and Tom were sceptical about this claim but chose not to argue with Sam about it, especially since they all believed that Fisher was not that far away anyway.

During the previous evening they had dried out their neckerchiefs and then spent most of their time stripping down their guns and cleaning them. They now seemed satisfied that they were once again functional and reliable. Cobb tested his rifle by firing into the lake. Luckily, despite their enforced swim, none of them had lost any of their ammunition.

'Now the question is where is Fisher?' said Cobb. 'As far as we know, the last we knew of him he was among those rocks over there. I suppose that's where we'd better start looking. Sam, this is where your knowledge of tracking really becomes useful.'

'I'll do my best,' said Sam. 'I ain't no expert though.'

'I'll make allowances for that,' said Cobb. 'The best thing you and me can do Tom, is to keep him covered while he looks.'

There was no obvious sign of Fisher as Sam set about scouring amongst the rocks for tracks, but Cobb could not help but feel that he was not too far away and possibly even watching them. Eventually Sam declared that he was reasonably certain that Fisher had moved up amongst the trees immediately behind the rocks. Cobb was slightly disappointed at this observation as it seemed obvious to him. However, he did not criticize Sam for discovering the obvious.

Sam moved slightly ahead of them and studied the ground closely and eventually stated that Fisher had most definitely climbed up an almost sheer bank about forty foot high. This time Cobb had to confess that he could not see anything to indicate this.

'Keep going, Sam,' said Cobb, trying to be as encouraging as possible. 'That looks one hell of a steep climb though, are you sure?'

'Sure, I'm sure,' said Sam. 'Look at this.' He indicated a small scuff mark on a rock about four feet off the ground. 'Made by his boot I'd say.'

'Or an animal of some kind,' said Tom.

'Animals don't wear boots,' said Sam. 'This is too steep for deer an' it sure don't look like mountain-goat country to me, they prefer more rocky places than this. No, sir, he went this way all right.'

'You keep on climbing, Sam,' suggested Cobb. 'Me and Tom will see if there's an easier way up.'

However, look as they might, there was no easier way up, in fact either side of that point it became much harder. Eventually they both returned and started to follow Sam who by that time had reached what looked like the top. He looked down on them with a broad smile across his face. He apparently found their efforts at climbing quite funny.

'He was up here all right,' Sam announced, as Cobb struggled on to the narrow ledge. 'There's a cave an' it looks like he spent the night there. I said he had a fire an' it's still warm.'

'Any sign of anything else?' asked Cobb.

'Nope, not a thing,' said Sam. 'All I know is that he went that way when he left.' He pointed along the ledge to Cobb's right.

'OK, Sam,' said Cobb. 'You're in charge, we'll follow you.'

'Yes, sir,' said Sam, quite proudly.

He led them along the narrow ledge which, after about half a mile, widened out and then blended with the surroundings. The trees had also become thicker and even Cobb had no difficulty in seeing Fisher's tracks amongst the fallen leaf litter. It seemed quite obvious that Fisher considered any attempt to cover his tracks would be useless and that he was apparently more intent on making as much headway as possible.

'Don't know if it means anythin', Major,' said Sam after some time, as they still followed the tracks, 'but it strikes me that we is goin' round in a circle. When we started out the sun was on our right an' now it's on our left.'

Cobb looked up at the sun shining through the trees and nodded. 'I must admit that I hadn't noticed,' he said, 'but yes, you're right. Where the hell is he leading us? A man like Fisher doesn't normally do things without a reason.'

'And I think the reason is that he's going back to the canoe,' said Tom. 'Since he ain't got no horse he'd be stupid to rely on out-runnin' us. Yep, I reckon he's led us right round just so's he can get to that canoe.'

'Hell!' exclaimed Cobb. 'You're probably right, Tom. I should have thought he'd do something like that. Sam, have you any idea how far away from the lake and the canoe we are?'

'No, not really,' admitted Sam. 'I reckon it's more or less straight ahead though, but don't ask me how far.'

'Then forget about following him,' said Cobb. 'We have to get to that canoe before he does.'

'OK, Major,' said Sam. 'Follow me. I'm sure we can't be too far away.'

'It could be a trap,' warned Cobb. 'Maybe he wants us to think he's going back for the canoe. Keep your eyes open and listen for any sounds.'

'That's goin' to slow us down a bit,' said Sam.

'I know, but we don't have much choice,' said Cobb.

Sam's sense of direction was accurate and after about fifteen minutes they found themselves at the side of the lake. The only problem was that it was not at the place where they had left the canoe.

'Which way?' asked Cobb.

'Your guess is as good as mine,' said Sam. 'You decide, Major.'

Cobb looked about and then ran to a

small outcrop of rock which he climbed and once again looked about. Eventually he pointed to his right.

'I seem to remember that big boulder down there,' he called. 'Yes, I'm quite certain it's that way.'

'I reckon it's as good a way as any,' said Tom. 'Let's go.'

Cobb had made the correct choice but they were too late. The canoe, containing Fisher, was already about fifty yards out into the lake but about 200 yards from where they were. All three stopped and raised their rifles and fired at the canoe, but their shots fell well short. They raced along the shoreline until they had reached the spot where they had camped, but by that time the canoe was plainly well out of range. All they could do was watch and curse as Fisher pulled further away.

'What the hell do we do now, Major?' asked Tom. 'Maybe we should have made sure he couldn't use the canoe.'

'But we didn't,' said Cobb. 'Damn, we almost had him.'

'The man said it was about thirty miles round the lake to Florence,' observed Sam. 'I guess we don't have much choice but to start walkin'.'

'By which time Fisher will be so far ahead of us we'll never catch him,' said Cobb. 'Still, as you say, Sam, we don't have much choice.'

9

Rather dejectedly, they started to walk along the edge of the lake all the time keeping watch on the progress of Fisher and regretting a lost opportunity. Eventually Fisher's canoe had become lost on the surface of the lake. They had been following round the edge of what turned out to be a small headland when, quite suddenly, Sam stopped and pointed.

'Somebody in a canoe!' he exclaimed. 'Maybe we won't have to walk.'

Sure enough there was a canoe being paddled towards them. Although it was fairly close inshore, it was still about 300 or 400 yards away. Immediately they started to run towards it waving their arms and calling out. It seemed to take an age for the canoe to come any closer but it was apparent that they had been seen as the figure in the canoe acknowledged them. Eventually it beached and the elderly man they had met in Florence slowly climbed out.

'I figured that maybe you could do with some help,' said the old man.

'You must be a mind-reader,' said Cobb. 'Fisher took us round in a circle and gave us the slip. I'm sorry to say your canoe sank. Fisher filled it full of holes. How the hell did you know we were in trouble?'

'I didn't, leastways not until I saw Fisher headin' back across the lake,' said the old man. 'I guess you could say I had this feelin', 'specially after I heard shootin' last night. We all heard it, but we had no way of knowin' if it was you shootin' at Fisher or Fisher shootin' at you.'

'You heard the shooting right across there?' queried Cobb.

'Sure thing,' said the old man. 'Sound travels a hell of a long way over water. I started out first thing this mornin'. I figured that I'd better come across, just in case you was in trouble. I was even prepared to take your bodies back.'

'Well whatever the reason, we sure are glad to see you,' said Tom. 'We'd just started to walk all the way round.'

'An' that's one hell of a walk,' said the old man. 'I knows a couple of fellers what did it a few years ago. There's a big marsh you have to cross an' it ain't easy. The name's Jake, by the way. OK, c'mon, Fisher has a good start an' I doubt me if he'll hang about too long. I hear tell he's likely as not headin' further down the lake to a place called Clark Hill. That's about forty miles away.'

'I won't ask how you found that out,' said Cobb. 'Just get us across as fast as possible. I'll see to it that you are paid for the loss of your canoe.'

Ten minutes later they were paddling as fast as they could across the lake towards Florence. Jake had anticipated that they might need extra paddles and had provided one each.

However, there was no way they were

able to make much headway on Fisher and by the time they were halfway, Jake pointed ahead.

'He's made it,' he announced. 'Don't you worry none though, there's only three ways he can leave Florence. He can head north, but that way is anythin' but easy an' he has to cross that marsh I was tellin' you about. He can head back the way you came in — that's probably the easiest way — but my money is still on him goin' south towards Clark Hill. From there it's about a two-day ride to the railroad out at Booneville. Where he goes after that is anybody's guess. It could be east, west or north. There's a main east to west railroad through Booneville but there's also a line from there up north. I don't know where that goes to. Anyhow, I've told the folk in Florence to keep an eye on which way he does go.'

'I can't see a thing,' said Tom. 'You must have damn good eyesight.'

'Not too bad,' agreed Jake. 'It's just the way things are, how used you are to lookin' for things. Out here a kid learns to recognize a canoe from a long way off almost before he can walk.'

As they paddled across the lake, although Jake did not ask, Cobb felt that he owed him an explanation and told him about the gold and the money.

'Ain't that much money in the whole world,' said Jake. 'One hundred thousand dollars. No, sir, there just ain't that much. Most I ever seen in one place is fifty dollars an' that was more'n three years ago, an' believe me there's plenty round these parts what'd kill a man for half that. Man, even ten dollars is a fortune in these parts. Most folk don't see more'n fifty dollars in a whole year an' talkin' in numbers over a hundred don't mean a thing to 'em other than it's a hell of a lot. Most folk ain't never had no real schoolin', see.'

'Well, that's how much it is,' said Cobb. 'How do you think he was able to offer those men a thousand dollars to kill us?'

'That's what they said he'd offered

'em,' said Jake. 'Didn't believe a word of it m'self. I told 'em they was mad if they believed him. No man pays out that kind of money when he could get the same job done for ten or twenty dollars. But they wouldn't listen. Mind, them two wouldn't never listen to sense.'

'I don't think he would have paid 'em,' said Sam. 'Only payment they would've got was the same as McGovan got, a bullet in the head.'

'More'n like,' agreed Tom. 'How much longer is this goin' to take? My arms just ain't used to this kind of work.'

'Keep paddling!' ordered Cobb. 'If we lose him now we're never going to get another chance.'

In fact it took them the best part of an hour before they were able to leap out of the canoe. Jake immediately asked the folk gathered round which way Fisher had gone. They all indicated down the lake.

'Where are our horses?' demanded Cobb.

'Don't you worry none, they is safe,' said Jake. 'Over in that paddock behind my place.' He indicated a rather run-down cabin about a hundred yards along the lake. 'Your saddles is in my cabin.'

'How far did you say it was to this Clark Hill?' asked Cobb.

'Forty miles,' said Jake. 'The goin' ain't too bad, not at this time of year anyhow. Most of the rivers runnin' into the lake are low an' easy to cross an' there ain't no big river between here an' Clark Hill.'

'Is there a shorter way?' asked Tom.

'Sure is,' said Jake. 'I wouldn't waste my time with it though. You need to be a mountain goat to go that way. Straight up an' straight down. It might be ten or fifteen miles shorter but it'll take you more'n twice as long an' then you need to know the way, which you don't.'

'You said he'd probably head for Booneville after Clark Hill,' said Cobb. 'Is there anywhere else he could go and is there another way to Booneville?'

'Only other way to Booneville is straight over the mountains,' said Jake. 'That'll take twice as long as goin' through Clark Hill. Fisher has the same choice if he wants to reach the railroad. There's a town called Bassett but that's about five days due south. Anyhow, if he does head that way it's south from Clark Hill an' Booneville is west. You'll soon find out which way he went.'

'What about Scottsboro?' asked Cobb.

'Not from this side of the lake,' said Jake. 'From here it's the best part of two hundred miles. From the other side, it's almost half that. Even if he does decide to head that way, he's still got to go through Clark Hill an' then take the road south for maybe forty miles or more.'

'Then I suppose we have to go through Clark Hill,' said Cobb.

They saddled their horses and were somewhat surprised to discover that the contents of their saddle-bags were still intact. It was not at all unusual for things to go missing even in the larger towns. Cobb handed Jake two ten-dollar bills.

'That should cover the cost of your canoe and your time,' he said. 'If we catch Fisher I might even ride out here and give you some more.'

'Hell, Marshal,' said Jake. 'Canoes don't cost much. Just a few branches an' some deer hide, that's all. Still, thanks all the same. It'll go in my tin for when I finally hang up my boots. I might even take me a ride into Booneville one day. I hear tell they got a saloon there where you can get yourself one of them real fancy women an' as much beer or whiskey as any man could want.'

'And that's one sure way of losing all your money,' warned Cobb. 'OK, thanks once again for your trouble, Jake. Maybe I'll see you again.'

'Probably not, Marshal,' said Jake. 'Florence is a nice place in its own way, but as far as most folk are concerned it might as well be up on the moon. In fact, Captain Fisher was the first man I ever met who came here more'n once. Couldn't really see why at the time, I mean, there must be thousands of other places to go fishin'. Still, now I know why, don't I? Best of luck, Marshal, I hope you catch him before somebody else finds out how much he's got an' kills him first. The kind of money you're talkin' about would tempt even Parson Jones an' they say nothin' can ever tempt him.'

'I hope we get to him first as well, Jake,' said Cobb, 'I'd hate to lose it after all we've been through.'

By that time Fisher had had about a two-hour start on them and they had no doubt that he would be riding fast to put as much ground between him and them as possible. Fisher also had the advantage of having some knowledge of the area.

The more he thought about it, the more Cobb was convinced that Fisher's apparent flight across the lake had been something he had planned for. It seemed to have been a quite deliberate and well-planned operation.

To Cobb's mind, Fisher had never had any intention of going across the lake in the normal course of events. It had been nothing more than a means of drawing off anyone following him should the need arise. In that respect it had worked perfectly. The only thing Fisher had not allowed for was the unpredictable human element, in this case in the form of Jake.

In many ways, Cobb was forced to admire the apparent efficiency with which Fisher had thought things through and his organization. He had allowed for the fact that somebody just might discover where he was going, hence the diversion by canoe. Bearing that in mind, Cobb was now quite convinced that Fisher had also made allowances for even that diversion to go wrong. He knew that it was more than possible that they would meet further trouble. He did not disclose his fears to either Tom or Sam.

Although the terrain was fairly flat

alongside the lake, it was impossible to travel with any speed. The strip closer to the lake, about twenty yards wide, although the flattest, was made up of rocks and small boulders which forced the horses to pick their way very slowly. The area between the foreshore and the forest provided the easiest route although even here they were forced to twist and turn amongst even larger boulders. They tried briefly riding through the edge of the forest but this proved more difficult. They eventually elected to keep to the strip between the foreshore and the forest.

Once or twice Sam pointed to scuff marks in the ground and seemed quite certain that they were made by Fisher's horse. Both Cobb and Tom were not quite so certain, especially when they came upon a small group of deer which left marks almost identical to those which Sam had claimed to have been made by Fisher. However, it appeared most likely that Fisher had gone that way. Indeed it appeared impossible to go any other way.

Their slow progress meant that they were forced to spend the night camped by the lake, but Cobb drew some consolation from the fact that Fisher had probably been forced to do the same. After some discussion it was decided that they might as well light a fire and not to post a lookout. Their meal consisted of some dried salt pork and beans and a mug of indifferent coffee. Sam did volunteer to hunt some fresh meat but they decided against it, mainly because Cobb did not want gunfire to attract unnecessary attention.

About two hours after starting out the following morning, they came across the first real indication that Fisher had indeed gone that way. They were crossing a small river when Sam, who was in the lead, suddenly stopped and pointed down at the mud and the clear imprint of a horse having passed that way.

'Not too long ago either,' asserted Sam.

'Long enough,' said Cobb. 'Still, at least we seem to be on the right trail. Considering how Fisher appears to have planned for every possibility, I suggest that from now on we be prepared for an ambush.'

'Me an' Sam had been prepared all along,' said Tom. 'He could've been hidden almost anywhere ever since we left Florence. I wonder how far this Clark Hill place is?'

'It shouldn't be too far now,' said Cobb, 'but I don't really know. As far as I'm concerned distance and time have very little meaning out here.'

'I reckon we is more'n halfway,' said Sam. 'Fisher might even be there now.'

'Or he might be waiting round the next bend,' warned Cobb.

They had several false alarms. Two were groups of deer and one turned out to be a particularly large and mean-looking bear. The bear appeared to be in no hurry to move and held them up for at least an hour despite them firing in an attempt to scare it.

As they rounded a small headland shortly after midday, Sam suddenly grabbed at his rifle and leapt off his horse, Tom and Cobb immediately did the same without question.

'Somebody up ahead!' whispered Sam. 'I heard voices.'

'Which probably means it ain't Fisher,' said Cobb. 'Unless he's taken to talking to himself.'

'I hear folk do just that,' said Sam. 'Makes it sound like company.'

'I can't hear nothin',' said Tom. 'Even if it ain't Fisher it could be that he's paid somebody to look out for us like he did before. I wouldn't trust nobody in these parts. I think most would sell their own for a couple of dollars, so a stranger don't have no chance.'

'I wouldn't trust them either,' agreed Cobb. 'Are you sure you heard somebody, Sam? I can't hear them.'

'I heard 'em,' asserted Sam. 'Can't hear 'em now though, but they is there all right.'

'Then I suggest that we go forward

on foot,' said Cobb. 'Be ready to start shooting.'

They moved forward slowly and quietly leading their horses and at first there was nobody to be seen. However, as they rounded a large boulder, they were suddenly faced with two men, one a white man and the other an Indian. There were two mules grazing nearby.

The two men did not appear too surprised to see them but wisely, seeing that they were outgunned, did not attempt to go for their guns which were on the mules. For a few moments each group stared at the other.

'Deputy US Marshal Cobb,' said Cobb. 'Have you seen a lone white man pass this way recently?'

For a brief moment the two men glanced at each other. That glance was sufficient to tell Cobb that they had seen Fisher.

'Nope,' drawled the white man, a rather dirty-looking man with a full beard. 'We been here two days now an' we ain't seen nobody 'ceptin' you.'

'Impossible!' snapped Cobb. 'We know that he came this way and not too long ago, certainly within the last three hours. You must have seen him.'

'Not necessarily,' responded the white man. 'We is fur trappers, see? We could've been out either settin' or checkin' our traps. A man could slip by without bein' seen if'n he wanted to.'

'Possibly,' conceded Cobb. 'How far is it to Clark Hill?'

'Four hours, maybe five,' said the man.

'And you are quite certain that you haven't seen anyone?' said Tom.

'I said so, didn't I?' said the man.

'Captain John Fisher,' said Cobb. 'He's the man we are after. Do you know him?'

'Never heard of him,' said the man. 'We spends most of our time out here an' you is the first folk we've seen out this way in more'n a year.'

'OK,' sighed Cobb, as he turned and whispered to Tom and Sam. 'They might be telling the truth but I have this feeling they are not. Mount up but be ready for them. It could be that Fisher has paid them.'

'Four or five hours, you say,' Tom said to the man. 'Is there a quicker way?'

'Nope,' said the man, spitting a wad of something on to the ground. 'You got three rivers to cross, easy enough, there ain't much water in 'em. Clark Hill is about half an hour after the third one. Can't miss it, ain't no other way to go.'

They rode slowly past the two men and Cobb noted that as they did so, both men moved towards their mules. Cobb nodded at both Tom and Sam and all three suddenly turned and fired.

The Indian fell to the ground still clutching an ancient rifle. The white man also jerked backwards, the rifle he had in his hand firing harmlessly into the air. Cobb immediately leapt off his horse, closely followed by Sam and Tom. He ran to the white man while Sam and Tom checked the Indian. The Indian was dead but the white man was still gasping for breath.

'He paid you to kill us, didn't he?' demanded Cobb.

'Fifty dollars!' rasped the old man. 'Said that somebody might be followin' him. Fifty dollars he paid us.'

'The going rate has come down quite a lot,' said Cobb. 'How long ago?'

'Two hours,' croaked the man. 'Said we'd get another fifty when we took your bodies to Clark Hill.'

'And you believed him?' asked Tom. 'He'd've been long gone.'

'Chance we had to take,' rasped the man. 'Fifty dollars apiece is a lot of money, easy money, too.'

'If you call dying for it easy money,' said Cobb. 'Did he say anything else? Did he give any indication that he knew who we were?'

'Nope,' the man rasped again. His eyes suddenly stared and then closed. His head lolled to one side.

'Two hours,' said Tom. 'He can't be that far ahead.'

'Two hours out here is a long way,'

said Sam. 'He's got the advantage as well. He could be waitin' anywhere to pick us off. What we goin' to do about these two? We can't just leave their bodies here.'

'I suppose we'll have to take them to Clark Hill,' said Cobb. 'Search them; they should have at least fifty dollars on them.'

However, they did not have the opportunity to search either body as a bullet suddenly ricocheted off a large rock, very close to Cobb's head. Immediately all three crashed to the ground seeking what cover they could. There was another shot this time rather more accurate in that it grazed Sam's head, but did not appear to do too much damage. Apart from the fact that the shots came from somewhere amongst the trees further up the slope, there was no indication as to exactly where they did come from.

'You might as well give yourself up, Fisher!' called Cobb. 'We managed to track you this far and the authorities know where we are.'

'I don't think they do,' called Fisher. 'So, it was you, Major Cobb. They said back in Florence that your name was Cobb but that you were a US marshal. Have you promoted yourself? I can't see why you should be bothered about the gold.'

'Deputy marshal,' corrected Cobb. 'They made me up when they asked me to come after you. As for the gold, let's just say that ten per cent of everything we recover is reason enough.'

'And the other two with you are Sam Coltrane and Tom Williams, I take it?' called Fisher 'My congratulations to you. I obviously made a mistake in thinking that you wouldn't bother. I won't ask how the hell you managed to track me this far, I obviously made a mistake of some kind. I thought I'd covered my tracks pretty well. I knew they would have difficulty in raising anyone to come after me but I must admit that I did not reckon on it being you. You didn't strike me as the type

221

who went in for bounty hunting.'

'We all have to make a living,' said Cobb. 'Let's just say that we did trace you. I must admit that it was a well-planned operation, even down to anticipating that somebody would follow and then forcing them to cross the lake. You just didn't reckon on a man like old Jake though. Those two Indians you paid and McBurney at the trading post weren't up to much either. By the way, we found McGovan's body as well.'

'You have been busy, Major,' said Fisher, with a somewhat derisive laugh. 'But then I shouldn't be too surprised, you are, like me, an experienced organizer. We would have made a good team. However, Major, it is not I who should give up, it is you. I know exactly where the three of you are, but you cannot see me. For the moment you are well covered, but should one of you so much as move a muscle I'll be able to see it and shoot you.'

'You can't stay there for ever,' said Cobb.

'I can certainly stay longer than you and long enough to pick you off one at a time, Major,' said Fisher with another derisive laugh. 'My plans are very flexible and I am free to move about as I please but you are not. Let us just see who lasts the longest. Oh, and don't get any ideas about one of you somehow managing to sneak up on me. I can assure you that I am ready for just such an eventuality, even down to one of you thinking he can get round by taking to the water.'

Cobb slowly raised his head, hoping to locate Fisher, but his effort was rewarded by a bullet ricocheting off a rock close to his head and he was forced to lie flat.

'Either of you two see where he is?' he called to Sam and Tom.

'Not exactly,' replied Sam. 'Best I can say is that he's in them trees.'

'Then it looks like we have a long wait,' said Cobb. He called to Fisher again. 'I hope you know that they don't like anybody killing a marshal, Fisher.'

'First they have to prove that I have,' said Fisher with another laugh. 'The chances of anybody finding your bodies out here are pretty remote.'

'There's just one thing I'd like to know,' called Tom. 'Why the hell didn't you finish us off when we were in the water when you sank the canoe?'

'Unfortunately, I must confess that that was down to nothing more than bad planning on my part,' replied Fisher. 'In my haste to get across the lake I forgot to take extra bullets for my rifle and a handgun was not much use at that distance. My bad luck, your good luck.'

There was a couple more shots as one of them moved but that apart there appeared to be no real effort by Fisher to move in for the kill.

Cobb managed to glance at his pocket watch several times and, just as the sun was setting behind the hills, he worked out that they had been lying there for more than five hours. Eventually, just as the darkness really started to close in, Cobb again raised his head. This time there was no shot.

'Either he can't see us now or he's gone,' Cobb said to the others. 'Does anybody feel brave enough to make a move?'

'Give it a mite longer,' advised Sam. 'When it's completely dark.'

Fifteen minutes later, all three slowly raised themselves, fully expecting to be shot at. However, their fears proved unfounded.

'I reckon he's moved on,' said Sam. 'Cover me, I'm goin' to take a look where he was.'

A few minutes later Sam returned to announce that there was no sign of Fisher.

'That doesn't mean that he's not far away,' warned Cobb.

'I think Sam's right,' said Tom. 'He's moved out. What do we do now, Major?'

'We follow,' said Cobb.

'In the dark!' exclaimed Tom. 'There's no knowin' where he'll be. I

225

say we wait until the mornin'. He can't travel too far or too fast, not in the dark.'

'Maybe you're right,' sighed Cobb. 'OK, we leave at dawn. No fire though, we don't want to present him with an easy target.'

10

Despite their worst fears and several false alarms, mainly caused by animals of one kind or another coming down to the lake to drink, their journey through to Clark Hill proved singularly uneventful. Cobb was forced to confess that he had expected Fisher to lie in wait for them somewhere along the route.

They had loaded the bodies of the two trappers on to their mules but they had left a pile of recently fleshed hides which were swarming in flies. They had also found fifty dollars in the pocket of the white man and Cobb decided to take charge of it as part of the stolen money.

Whether or not their arrival in Clark Hill — a group of shacks and much the same size as Florence — was expected, was very difficult to determine at first. Most of the population, again a mix of roughly half and half white and Indian or half-breed, appeared more concerned about the two bodies brought in. There were a few mutterings, particularly amongst the Indians, some of them almost threatening. However, on seeing Cobb's badge of office, the threats seemed to disappear although the mutterings remained. Both bodies were claimed by two elderly Indian women.

'There was a white man through here, either during the night or early this morning,' said Cobb to a group of men. 'Name of Fisher, Captain Fisher. Which way did he go?'

'We ain't seen nothin', Marshal,' grunted one of the white men. 'If he did come through here he must've passed through durin' the night. Come to think of it my dog barked sometime in the middle of the night an' he don't usually do that, not even when we get bears through.'

'That's 'cos dogs know bears'll eat 'em,' said another man. 'Sure, my dog was mighty restless too for a while. He don't normally bother if it was just a bear or even a wolf.'

'What time was that?' asked Cobb.

'Time, Marshal?' said the first man with a wry smile. 'All I can say is it was dark so it was the middle of the night. Old Silas Gray's got himself a timepiece, maybe he can tell you.'

'Naw!' said the second man. 'He wouldn't know either. He might have a timepiece but he can't read the time. He only bought it for show when he went to Booneville once.'

'Booneville,' said Cobb. 'Which way is that?'

'Straight up the valley,' said the first man. 'Just keep goin' for two days.'

'What do you think?' Cobb asked Tom and Sam. 'Booneville, Scottsboro or somewhere called Bassett. I think he was probably heading for Booneville and the railroad, but he might have changed his mind.'

'Or he might want you to think he's changed his mind,' said Tom. 'I'm with you, I think he went to Booneville.'

'Well either these folk don't know or won't say,' said Cobb. 'Let's go. As far as we know Fisher must have travelled all night which gives him one hell of a good start. We've got a lot of ground to make up.'

'Major,' said Tom, 'there's somethin' don't make much sense to me. Fisher had us pinned down last night and could've taken us out one at a time almost anywhere along the trail. Why didn't he? OK, I'll buy that bit about forgettin' his bullets when he sank the canoe, but not this time.'

'On account of he didn't want to?' suggested Sam.

'Naw,' said Tom. 'I think he wanted to all right. Sure, we was well covered last night an' he wouldn't take the risk in the dark, but this mornin' was different. Any other man would've waited for us.'

'I tend to agree,' said Cobb. 'He had the advantage and could easily have killed us along the trail. Since I also agree that it was not because he didn't want to, I am forced to conclude that he didn't because he simply did not have the time for some reason.'

'You mean that he had to get to Booneville to catch a train?' said Tom.

'That would seem most likely,' said Cobb. He spoke to the group of men again. 'Is there a quicker way to Booneville?'

'Shorter, sure,' replied one of them. 'Quicker though? Well, that all depends on the weather. It could be you is lucky though, this is the dry time of the year an' this year it's drier than usual. You could make Booneville in just over a day.'

'We'll chance it,' decided Cobb. 'Which way?'

'Straight through the valley, maybe an hour from here,' said the man. 'Main trail goes straight on, you can't miss it. At the end of the valley you'll see a big old pine, huge tree it is, again you can't miss it. Up to the right of the pine you'll see a big boulder, almost looks like a small mountain but it ain't. Go round behind that an' you'll see a gully. Should be dry at this time of year so you should get through OK. After that keep two tall peaks directly ahead of you. Once you reach them you'll see Booneville down below you. There's a couple of places where you'll have to get off your horses an' lead 'em. You'll soon see why.' He did not elaborate and Cobb chose not to ask.

Finding the tree and the boulder was easy enough. The gully proved to be dry and it was not too long before they were winding their way steadily upwards towards the two peaks.

As was quite normal, distances proved quite deceptive and they were forced to make camp some time before they reached the peaks. Again their meal consisted of dried salt pork and beans. There was no shortage of clear pools of water and enough grass and shrubbery to satisfy their horses. That night proved to be the coldest they had spent thus far and a fire was kept burning all night.

The following morning they discovered exactly what the man had meant about having to lead their horses. They had to negotiate two narrow ledges, each no more than three feet wide. Cobb was terrified of heights but managed to keep his fear under control. It was not until they were all safely across the second ledge that he discovered both Sam and Tom had exactly the same fear. After that the going was quite easy. It was almost midday when they found themselves looking down on a green plain and what was obviously the town of Booneville.

'At least it's a decent-sized town,' said Cobb. 'They should have a sheriff and he should have been told to look out for Fisher.'

'Which makes me wonder if he's here,' said Tom. 'Surely he wouldn't head for a place where he knew they'd be lookin' out for him. I know I wouldn't. I wouldn't be surprised if he's given us the slip.'

'Unfortunately you could be right,' said Cobb. 'That, however, is a chance we'll have to take.'

'Major,' said Sam, 'I don't mean to tell you how to do your job, but if Fisher is there, don't you think it'd be better if he didn't know we was about too? One smell of us an' he'll like as not make a run for it.'

'You are not as dumb as they say you are, Sam,' said Cobb. 'You are right. I must admit that I hadn't really thought about that. OK, since it was you who had the bright idea, what do you suggest we do about it?'

'Well, we have to get down first,' said Sam. 'Looks easy enough though. Then I suggest that we head for the nearest ranch, farm or homestead an' get someone from there to ride into town an' bring the sheriff out to us.'

'Brilliant! Quite brilliant,' said Cobb. 'That's just what we'll do.'

Once down on level ground, they soon came across a farmhouse where they found a middle-aged man and two younger men who turned out to be his sons, doing some weeding. Cobb explained to the man why they could not just ride into Booneville. The man agreed to send one of his sons to the sheriff.

It took almost an hour for the boy to return with Sheriff Wilson, a man about the same age as Cobb. At first the sheriff looked at him suspiciously and was only satisfied that Cobb was who he claimed to be when Cobb produced his authorization document.

'OK, Marshal,' said the sheriff. 'What's so hell-fire important that you can't just ride into town?'

'Captain John Fisher,' said Cobb. 'Weren't you informed that he had stolen abut fifty thousand in gold and another fifty thousand in cash? I was assured that all law enforcement agencies had been notified.'

'Never heard a thing,' said the sheriff. 'Nothin' at all unusual in that though. Here at Booneville we're often the last to hear about things like that. Fifty thousand in cash and fifty thousand in gold, that's a hell of a lot of money.'

'Which is why we are after him,' said Cobb.

'And what makes you think he headed this way?' asked the sheriff.

Cobb explained what had happened since they had left Geraldine and the sheriff seemed convinced.

'Have you had any strangers in Booneville in the past few hours?' asked Cobb. 'Possibly this morning. We know he can't be that far ahead of us.'

'Marshal,' said the sheriff. 'Booneville is on the main railroad. We often get strangers through for various reasons. I don't take too much notice of them though. If I did I'd never get any other work done. If your man has come in to catch a train then he'll have to wait until six o'clock tonight. Last one was yesterday morning. I was there when it pulled out and as far as I can remember only three people caught it out and only two came in.'

'Of course it could be that he has given us the slip,' conceded Cobb. 'I think he did come this way though.'

'What do you want me to do?' asked the sheriff.

'Ride back into town and keep an eye open for him,' said Cobb. 'You wouldn't be noticed, but he knows who we are.'

'And if I come across somebody who could be him?'

'Send somebody out here and we'll take it from there,' said Cobb. He called the farmer in and explained the position. 'Do you mind if we wait here?'

'Sure thing,' agreed the farmer. 'I just don't want no trouble here though. I've got my wife an' family to consider.'

'There will be no trouble,' assured Cobb. 'OK, Sheriff, we'll wait for you.'

It was just over two hours when one of the sheriff's deputies rode up to the farm and told them that Sheriff Wilson thought that he had located Fisher.

'He's in the Golden Steer Hotel,' said the deputy. 'The sheriff says that he's made some enquiries and that your man seems to be waiting for somebody. If he is, he reckons he'll be comin' in on the six o'clock train.'

Cobb looked at his pocket watch — 3.30 — and ordered Sam and Tom to mount up. The deputy led them into town and he had obviously been told to take a back route. The three of them were eventually ushered through the rear door of the sheriff's office.

'He hasn't left the hotel,' said Wilson. 'He's got a room at the front overlooking the railroad station. I can get you in round the back way if you want.'

'Your deputy said that he seemed to be waiting for somebody,' said Cobb. 'What makes you think that?'

'The hotel is owned by my brother-in-law,' said the sheriff. 'His name *is* Fisher which means he must be your man. He also told my sister that he was expecting a visitor and that when he arrived he was to be sent up to his room.'

'Waiting for somebody,' mused Cobb.

'I hadn't expected that. I wonder who it might be?'

'We could take Fisher and wait in his room,' suggested Tom.

'We could, but I'd rather wait and find out who and why,' said Cobb. 'You say you can get us into the hotel without being seen,' he said to the sheriff. 'Can you get us into a room close to his? Preferably one also overlooking the railroad station.'

'Leave it with me,' said the sheriff. I'm sure we can arrange something.'

Ten minutes later, the sheriff returned and announced that the room next to the one taken by Fisher was available. He then led them through a series of alleyways and eventually through the back door of the hotel. They managed to get into the room without being seen. By that time it was 4.30 and they settled down to wait for the arrival of the train. They took it in turns to keep watch on both the railroad station and the street.

They had been watching and waiting

for slightly less than an hour when they heard the door to Fisher's room open and close. Eventually they saw a figure which did prove to be Captain John Fisher walk out on to the street. He was not carrying any luggage.

'I'll search his room,' said Cobb. 'You two keep an eye open for him coming back. I'll see what I can find. Bang on the wall if he comes back.'

The room was locked and Cobb had to run down the stairs and get the pass key. At first the room appeared empty apart from Fisher's rifle which was propped up in the corner. At least it seemed that he intended to return. It did not take Cobb very long to find a fairly large, flat case under the mattress and, as expected, it contained what seemed to be bags of gold and considerable amounts of money. Suddenly there was a loud knock on the wall and rather than remove the case, Cobb decided to leave it where it was so that he could confront Fisher and whoever he was meeting with it. He knew enough to know that a man like him would turn the fact that it was missing to his advantage if necessary. He had just returned to the other room when they heard Fisher entering his room. It appeared that Cobb's search had gone unnoticed.

As was quite normal, the six o'clock train did not arrive until half past. Three people alighted and only one boarded, a young woman. The three alighting passengers appeared at the main entrance and immediately Cobb let out a gasp of surprise.

'Simon Jopson!' he exclaimed.

'Jopson?' queried Tom.

'Yes, Jopson,' said Cobb. 'He's the man who had me made up to deputy marshal. How the hell does he figure in this?'

'He's obviously in with Fisher,' said Tom.

'Then why the hell have me made a deputy marshal and send us off after Fisher?' said Cobb.

'Search me,' said Tom. 'None of this

has made much sense anyhow.'

'He's headin' towards the hotel,' announced Sam. 'He *must* be the one Fisher was expectin'. The other two have gone off up the street.'

A few minutes later they heard a knock on the door to Fisher's room and then a few muffled words. Cobb motioned the other two to remain silent for a while as he pressed his ear against the adjoining wall. He eventually shook his head.

'I can't hear what they're saying,' he said. 'Still, I think I've seen enough. We go in and find out just what is happening.'

'Sheriff Wilson is also heading this way,' said Sam. 'Do we wait for him?'

'No, we go in now!' said Cobb.

Cobb did not knock, he simply burst in, gun in hand, to confront Fisher and Jopson. Sam and Tom followed, also with guns at the ready.

'What the hell . . . ' exclaimed Jopson.

'To use your own phrase, Mr Jopson,

precisely what the hell is going on?' demanded Cobb. 'You are both under arrest.'

'I thought you said they'd been dealt with?' spluttered Jopson, glaring at Fisher.

'I thought so too,' said Fisher. 'I paid four men on the road from Clark Hill to kill him with the promise of more if they did. How the hell did you get here?'

'And it wasn't the first time you paid somebody, Captain Fisher,' said Cobb. 'Your choice of killers was bad. As you can see, they all failed.'

'How did you get here so soon?' asked Fisher. 'It's impossible.'

'You'd better believe your own eyes,' said Cobb. 'Sam, go tell the sheriff he's got some customers for his cells.'

'No need,' came a voice from behind them. 'I saw this feller come into the hotel and thought I'd better be on hand in case you wanted help.'

'And you arrived just in time, Sheriff,' said Jopson. 'I want you to arrest these men. I'm Simon Jopson and have authority to order their arrest. This man is pretending to be a deputy US marshal.'

'Nice try, Mr Jopson,' said the sheriff. 'I sent a wire to Geraldine asking what was going on. It appears that Major Cobb *is* who he claims to be and that Captain Fisher *is* a wanted man. I was supposed to have been notified about the theft of the gold and money, but it appears that for some reason Booneville was left off the list. I think you have a few questions to answer. I know there are some people in Geraldine who want some answers. It seems that another twenty thousand dollars has gone missing.'

'Look under the mattress, Sheriff,' said Cobb. 'You'll find a case. It contains the gold and the rest of the money.'

'And I reckon that bag you were carrying, Mr Jopson, should have the other twenty thousand,' said the sheriff. 'I'll take charge of it.'

The sheriff reached for the bag Jopson had been carrying when suddenly Jopson produced a small pistol which he aimed at the sheriff's head.

'Don't one of you move,' croaked Jopson. 'The first one who does kills the sheriff.'

'That was a stupid move, Mr Jopson,' said Cobb. 'There's three guns aimed at you. You so much as even look as though you're going to squeeze that trigger and you are a dead man. I'm quite sure you didn't come all this way just to die.'

'He's right, Jopson,' said Fisher. 'We had it all worked out but it failed. I for one do not intend dying for it.'

'Damn you, Cobb!' snarled Jopson. 'We had it all worked out between us. The one mistake we made was hiring you in the first place.'

'Then why did you make me up to deputy marshal?' asked Cobb. 'That part just doesn't make any sense at all.'

'Because I had no choice!' snarled Jopson. 'I had direct orders to offer you the position — damn them! That bit about having your discharge from the army reviewed was right. It would appear that you have friends in high places, *Major Cobb*.'

'If I do, I certainly don't know who they are,' said Cobb. 'Your planning was very good, Captain,' he continued. 'The pity is, at least from your point of view, that you didn't kill me yourself. It was a mistake to try and hire other men to do it for you. Mind you, it would seem that you learn fast. A thousand dollars the first time, and that only on the off-chance that you were being followed down to fifty dollars when you realized that folk out Florence way thought that even ten dollars was a fortune.'

'And all a waste of money,' said Fisher. 'OK, Jopson, hand that gun over to them. We tried and we failed. We both knew what would happen if things did go wrong.'

'And they started to go wrong from the day you hired Cobb to guard that sand,' muttered Jopson, handing the gun to Cobb.

'Just one thing, Major,' said Fisher. 'How did you get on to me? I am quite certain that I never mentioned any names or places to anyone.'

'Nobody except Sheriff McGovan,' said Cobb.

'He's dead,' said Fisher. 'I know he didn't have any place names written down on him.'

'But you forgot about Ed Bishop and Jack Crane,' said Cobb. 'They overheard you and McGovan talking. Well, not exactly everything you said, but they remembered Paynes Creek and Florence Wheeler. Paynes Creek was easy enough, that's where we found McGovan's body. From there, there was only one way you could go and that was through Harper City. I must admit that the name Florence Wheeler almost had us fooled. We thought it was the name of some woman, but we happened to mention it to the bartender in Harper City and he told us it was really the town of Florence on Lake Wheeler. Apparently he only knew that because his mother was born there. But for that, we would probably still be looking for you.'

'Damn the man and his mother,' said Fisher with a wry laugh. 'How the hell was I expected to plan for where a man's mother was born?'

*   *   *

Both Jopson and Fisher were kept under guard in the jail until the arrival of a train which would, after one change *en route*, take Fisher and Jopson back to Geraldine with Cobb, Sam and Tom acting as escort.

The actual amount of cash recovered amounted to just over $71,000. The value of the gold was eventually confirmed as just under $59,000, making a grand total of $130,000.

It transpired the whole idea had been thought up by Simon Jopson who was bitter at being passed over for higher office. Captain Fisher admitted that he had allowed himself to be talked into it.

In addition to the agreed ten per cent reward of $13,000, an additional reward of $2,000 was paid for the apprehension of both Jopson and Fisher.

'Five thousand dollars each,' Cobb said to Sam and Tom. 'I suppose this is the parting of the ways for us?'

'I'm afraid so,' said Tom. 'The most money I've ever had in my life before is one hundred and fifty dollars. I had my eye on a hardware store back in my home town of Bullhead. I reckon I'll go and see if it's still up for sale.'

'An' I'm off back home to see if my widder woman is still available,' said Sam. 'Buy myself a decent place where she can teach me to read an' write proper. How about you, Major?'

'Well, they have offered me the job of deputy marshal permanently,' said Cobb. 'I'm not sure that I fancy that idea too much though. True, the money they're offering isn't too bad and it does have the advantage of being regular, but on the other hand I don't really fancy the idea of chasing outlaws for the rest of my life.'

'You'd make a good marshal,' said Tom. 'But I know what you mean. Anyhow, whatever you choose, Major, I wish you the best of luck. Just don't ever think about askin' me to work for you again, that's all. The money might be good but the risks are too great.'

'Me neither,' said Sam. 'Oh, an' don't you worry none about me. I just proved to myself I don't need drink. I know that's goin' to please my widder woman.'

'It's all right,' assured Cobb. 'I have thought about it and I am not going to become a lawman. The money might be good but I think bounty hunting probably pays even better and it has the advantage that I can pick and choose when or if I work.'

'Bounty huntin!' both Tom and Sam exclaimed together.

'Major,' said Tom. 'I've known me a

couple of bounty hunters an' they both said they were probably more hated than the men they hunted. Both of 'em is dead now though.'

'It was just a thought,' said Cobb with a wry laugh.

Both Sam and Tom were not quite so certain that it *was* nothing more than a thought.

THE END

We do hope that you have enjoyed reading this large print book.

Did you know that all of our titles are available for purchase?

We publish a wide range of high quality large print books including:
Romances, Mysteries, Classics General Fiction Non Fiction and Westerns

Special interest titles available in large print are:
The Little Oxford Dictionary Music Book, Song Book Hymn Book, Service Book

Also available from us courtesy of Oxford University Press:
Young Readers' Dictionary (large print edition) Young Readers' Thesaurus (large print edition)

For further information or a free brochure, please contact us at:
Ulverscroft Large Print Books Ltd., The Green, Bradgate Road, Anstey, Leicester, LE7 7FU, England. Tel: (00 44) **0116 236 4325 Fax:** (00 44) **0116 234 0205**

RODEO RENEGADE

Ty Kirwan

When English couple Rufus and Nancy Medford inherit a ranch in New Mexico, they find the majority of their neighbours are hostile to strangers. Befriended by only one rancher, and plagued by rustlers, the thought of returning to England is tempting, but needing to prove himself, Rufus is coached as a fighter by a circus sharp shooter, the mysterious Ghost of the Cimarron. But will this be enough to overcome the frightening odds against him?

CABEL

Paul K. McAfee

Josh Cabel returned home from the Civil War to find his family all murdered by rioting members of Quantrill's band. The hunt for the killers led Josh to Colorado City where, after months of searching, he finally settled down to work on a ranch nearby. He saved the life of an Indian, who led him to a cache of weapons waiting for Sitting Bull's attack on the Whites. His involvement threw Cabel into grave danger. When the final confrontation came, who had the fastest — and deadlier — draw?

RIVERBOAT

Alan C. Porter

When Rufus Blake died he was found to be carrying a gold bar from a Confederate gold shipment that had disappeared twenty years before. This inspires Wes Hardiman and Ben Travis to swap horse and trail for a riverboat, the *River Queen*, on the Mississippi, in an effort to find the missing gold. Cord Duval is set on destroying the *River Queen* and he has the power and the gunmen to do it. Guns blaze as Hardiman and Travis attempt to unravel the mystery and stay alive.

McKINNEY'S LAW

Mike Stotter

McKinney didn't count on coming across a dead body in the middle of Texas. He was about to become involved in an ever-deepening mystery. The renegade Comanche warrior, Black Eagle, was on the loose, creating havoc; he didn't appear in McKinney's plans at all, not until the Comanche forced himself into his life. The US Army gave McKinney some relief to his problems, but it also added to them, and with two old friends McKinney set about bringing justice through his own law.

BLACK RIVER

Adam Wright

John Dyer has come to the insignificant little town of Black River to destroy the last living reminder of his dark past. He has come to kill. Jack Hart is determined to stop him. Only he knows the terrible truth that has driven Dyer here, and he knows that only he can beat Dyer in a gunfight. Ex-lawman Brad Harris is after Dyer too — to avenge his family. The stage is set for madness, death and vengeance.

Roscommon County Library Service

WITHDRAWN
FROM STOCK